Sequel to Waking Up in Graceland

Amazing Grace

An Elvis Story

Kelly Peach

to Sharlene the Elvis fan

READ often
be AMAZING
give GRACE.

Kelly :)

This is a work of fiction. Names, characters, places and incidents are either products of the author's imagination or used fictitiously. Any resemblance to actual events, locales or persons, living or dead, is entirely coincidental.

Cover design by Katie Robinson
Published in the United States by Piccadilly Peach Publishing, LLC
piccadillypeach.com
Printed in the United States of America
ISBN 978-0-692-13723-9
First paperback edition: October 2018

COMMENTS FROM THE ADVANCE TEAM

"What a sequel! A love triangle, history lesson and cautionary tale about what it means to follow your heart. Unexpected twists and turns amid avid attention to detail."
– Becky Reichardt, St. Louis, Missouri

"Grace is so spunky, sweet and funny. You'll fall in love and want to meet her!"
– Chris Scherting, St. Louis, Missouri

"A fun, suspenseful story that keeps you guessing. I loved it!"
– Joyce Romine, St. Louis, Missouri

"I was sucked into this book and could not put it down! I lost myself in Maggie's journey, especially her stolen moments with Elvis."
– Cindy Denner, Lakeland, Florida

"I enjoyed the suspense, as well as the Elvis and Graceland history that Kelly wove into the book."
– Kati Eddinger, Aurora, Illinois

FOR JIM McMULLAN

My friend from childhood who read Waking Up in Graceland
the day after it launched and left us too soon in 2017.
I miss you. Rest in peace.

P

#Undedicated

FOR MY READERS

You bless me with your enthusiasm and support.
The spirit of Elvis shimmies among us!

PROLOGUE

Baby, Let's Play House

Time for tea.

Natural light beaming from a tall window accentuated the colors of this playful space. Peach-hued walls embraced bedroom furniture with bold red accents. The bedspread, an orange floral explosion, added warmth while polka dots chimed in with whimsy.

A tiny table was set with cups and saucers, plates and utensils, in another assembly of warm tones that encircled a shapely teapot ready with its brew.

Five guests were seated at three small chairs. A baby doll shared her seat with a stuffed hound dog. An American Girl Doll, in hippy garb, held a teal blue teddy bear on her lap. Only the stuffed monkey sat solo, his long arms and legs dragging the floor. Perhaps all guests had not yet arrived; one chair remained to be filled.

A rustle came from behind a slightly ajar closet door where a light was on. Suddenly, the door was thrust wide open in a dramatic, attention-getting sweep that announced a little girl in a white cape.

She was crowned with bright blonde curls, brushed to one side and pinned back with a purple bow. Under the cape, this precious 4-year old was dressed for the occasion in a princess frock billowing with layers of tulle. Her smile revealed a single dimple on her left cheek. Her eyes, a heavenly blue, gave away a bubbly temperament.

"Good afternoon, everyone, and thanks for coming to Minnie Mae's Tea House," the little hostess said as she approached her guests. "We're going to enjoy some delicious teas and cakes. But first, let's meet the lucky guests who were invited to be here today."

Taking her position behind the empty chair, she motioned to the hippy doll. "Miss, if you could please begin."

The introductions were made by the hostess, using a variety of voices for her tea party characters.

"I'm Julie, and I'm proud to be an American Girl Doll. This is TC Bear; he's a little shy."

"Hi," was all the blue bear said.

In baby talk, the baby doll said, "My name is Pwisilla and I'm 1 year old."

"And I'm Jeffrey the hound dog," said the Basset hound, in the deepest voice the little girl could muster.

Finally, the monkey spoke up. "My name is Scatter and I like to swing from trees."

"Very good! Nice to meet you all!" the hostess exclaimed. "Allow me to introduce myself. My name is Grace Christina Coyle." She reached out with both arms to grab the ends of her bedazzled white cape, raising them upward like an angel spreading her wings. "You can call me *Amazing Grace*."

CHAPTER 1

Too Much

August 2011

So much has happened since I woke up in Graceland. It's time to share the stories!

After my "Elvis time-traveling" adventure in Memphis, I took Chris's advice and wrote it all down. He bought me a leather-bound journal and was supportive, even though I knew he didn't believe I went back to 1960 and hung out with the King of Rock 'n Roll.

I was a mess when I first returned to the present, trying to process the wild, abstract notion that I had somehow crossed through time. I was consumed with unanswered questions and a mad love for Elvis. Those three days and nights with him were a whirlwind. My journaling gained value with the passage of time. When I go back and read the pages now, the fog lifts from the details and feelings awaken in my heart.

I still wonder about the afternoon when Elvis woke up and I was gone from Graceland. Was he angry? Did he look for me? He probably just moved on. The guy had a serious amount of choices, including the young and beautiful Priscilla. My heart wants to believe that he missed me, at least a little bit.

I had my hands full of romance, too. Chris and I had instant crushes on each other that quickly blossomed into a loving relationship. He asked me out right away, the first night we were back in St. Louis. He took me to his favorite Italian restaurant and the more we talked, the more we realized we had an uncanny bond worth exploring. We became fast friends and our intimacy proved to be powerful, more than two people just hooking up. I may have been out of my mind, but I was falling in love.

We both fell in love, actually. It felt right, from the beginning, like we were meant to be. Our journey to Memphis, in search of a newspaper story, was supposed to happen. We make each other happy and have a lot of fun. My family likes him; Chris' family likes me. We handle the serious stuff together. He's a real partner in crime.

As time marched on after Graceland, I focused more on the present than the past. Dalai Lama says, "*There are only two days that nothing can be done: one is yesterday and the other is tomorrow.*" I knew I had to live for today.

I never gave up on Elvis, though. I tried to go back to him. Twice.

Like I said, so much has happened since I woke up in Graceland. Now it's time to TCB—*Take Care of Business.*

CHAPTER 2

Big Hunk O' Love

December 28, 2006

When we got back to St. Louis, Chris was in a big hurry to get to the newspaper and write his story. He drove straight to my house, put the car in park and grabbed his door handle to get out. I touched him on the arm. He stopped and looked back at me.

"Chris," I began, then hesitated because I was truly a scrambled brain of thoughts and emotions.

"Maggie," he jumped in. "Can we do this later? You know I have a deadline."

"What do you mean 'do this later'?" I asked a little testily, then recovered. "Never mind, I completely understand. Go. Write a wonderful, gripping account of our trip to Memphis and Elvis and …"

A kiss on the lips interrupted me in mid-sentence. Now it was his turn to be the aggressor. I had planted the first kiss on him the night before I woke up in Graceland. I closed my eyes and allowed his lips on mine as long as the moment would last—which wasn't long, because his mind was on other things. He withdrew his lips but his hands held my face close to his. We were nose to nose.

"We," Chris said with extra emphasis, "have a lot to talk about … and a lot to do." He punctuated that line with kisses to my forehead, nose and lips, then broke into an irresistible grin. "How about dinner tonight, after I finish my work?"

"That sounds like a good place to start," I replied. "Stomachs first." I noticed my heart rate had increased. It made me smile, knowing I must have a thing for this guy. Or at least his kisses.

"Let's get your bags and I'll walk you to the door. I'll call when I know what kind of timeframe I'll be on." We both got out of the car.

At the front door, I scrounged for my keys inside my purse. Chris put my bags down and grabbed my shoulders, rubbing them for a few seconds. He whispered in my ear, which made all the right nerves stand at attention. "Remember what I said, write it all down… everything you can remember that happened in Memphis." He kissed me on my ear. "Then we'll pick up where we left off."

I could have jumped his bones right there in front of my house, but when I pushed open the door and turned around, he was taking long strides to his car. He gave the horn a single honk and waved as he took off.

It felt good to be home. I picked up my cat, Scatter, to give her some love and shook off the wave of heat that Chris had awakened. Back to reality. I put a few things away and slipped into sweats. Then I took his advice—I curled up on the couch with a notebook and wrote furiously. I smiled at the coincidence that Chris was also busy composing his Elvis story.

We'd grown closer on our journey to Memphis, especially with the handholding and emotions of the return trip home. In no time, though, my thoughts transferred from the sexy "present day" reporter to the King of Rock 'n Roll.

CHAPTER 3

My Baby Left Me

December 31, 1960

A King never truly slumbers, not with the worries and demands of his kingdom. Unless His Majesty takes sleeping pills. In the world of Elvis Presley, an uncommon man with ceaseless energy that fluctuated between creativity and nervousness, a few pills had become the prescription for a good night's rest.

This day began like most others, in the late afternoon. A groggy Elvis slowly awakened, his stomach sending messages that it was time to eat. He reached for the house phone on his nightstand that would alert his team to get prepared, when it hit him: she was gone.

Elvis sat up, curious eyes searching his bedroom. Maggie must be in the bathroom. He lay back on the pillows, his unique lip-curling grin on his face. "Hey, Maggie the Moody girl," he bellowed, "Come here and give me some lovin'." No response. Maybe she's in the shower? Time for another cold-water wakeup call! Elvis hopped out of bed and dashed into the bathroom to pull a prank.

The shower wasn't running. She wasn't in here either. Feeling a little aggravated, Elvis went to the phone again and called downstairs. Alberta answered. "Happy New Year's Eve, Mr. Elvis, what can I fix up for you today?" she inquired dutifully from the kitchen.

"Send Maggie up here, will you, please, VO5?" he asked sternly yet using his nickname for his favorite cook and maid.

There was a moment of silence on the line then Alberta replied, "Mr. Elvis, Miss Maggie has not come down yet today."

"What!" Elvis exclaimed. "Let me talk to Red! Send him up here right now. Please."

Elvis threw a matching satin robe over his purple pajama pants while he waited for Red to arrive. Soon, there was a knock on his bedroom door. "Come in," he announced, standing at his bedside with his arms crossed.

Red walked in, his eyes immediately scanning the room for a problem. "What's up, E? Everything OK?"

"I can't find Maggie. She's not here. Alberta says she hasn't come down. Where else could she be? What do you know?" Elvis was impatient.

"Um, Elvis, I haven't seen her today either," Red said, hesitantly making eye contact with his boss. "Honest." A pause between the two. "Hey, um, I'll take a look in all of the other rooms up here. Maybe she's just wandering around." Red headed for the door.

"I'm coming with you." Elvis followed him around the second floor, including his office, dressing room, bathroom and spare bedrooms.

The search was fruitless. No Maggie. Elvis headed back into his bedroom, where he paced furiously. "Something's wrong, Red. She wouldn't just leave me like that." He stopped right in front of Red. "Something happened last night, and I want to know what. She came up here and was all red and crying. Somebody touched her, Red. In my goddamn house! She had blotches on her neck and I'm gonna make the bastard pay!"

At this, Red broke eye contact and looked at the floor. Elvis continued. "I went downstairs and took a look around last night but didn't see anybody. Red, I wanna know what happened. This is *my house*. Tell me what you know!"

Red looked away again, gathering his thoughts a moment, then looked Elvis in the eye. "I didn't see anything or anyone last night, Elvis. I'm sorry. I headed to my room the same time you went to yours," he said, hoping to sound convincing.

Elvis wasn't buying it. He paced back and forth, punching a fist into the palm of his other hand. Thinking. Growing angrier. Red could feel the heat coming from his boss. "Here's what you're gonna do, Red. You're gonna form a little search party and look inside every room and every building on this property. Get it going now and report back to me as soon as you can."

Red nodded and made for the door. But Elvis wasn't finished yet. "One more thing, Red. I don't know if Maggie's playing a joke or in some kind of trouble. Either way, I want you to take this seriously. I know you don't like her but I don't give a shit. She's special to me and I want her here where she's safe and I can keep an eye on her. Especially after whatever happened last night. You hear me?" Red nodded again and left the room. He didn't have the guts to tell Elvis that maybe Maggie just left him.

CHAPTER 4

I Forgot to Remember to Forget

December 30, 2006

I'm usually slow to wake up, but it didn't take long this morning because I knew there would be something waiting for me on the front lawn—the newspaper article about our trip to Graceland! What had begun with me pitching an Elvis story idea resulted in the paper sending Chris to Memphis with me. He'd taunted me with lame teasers since then. "Wait until you see what I wrote about you know what," or "Gosh, I hope my editor doesn't cut out the part where I describe … oh, never mind, we'll see what makes print." Thankfully, the paper published his story quickly, with cover placement in the weekend Lifestyles section.

With chants of "Extra, extra, read all about it" in my head, I scurried out of bed, stopping only briefly to make sure I had enough clothes on to leave the house. Scatter followed me and took the opportunity to dash for some outside time when I opened the front door.

The bundle was waiting on the lawn. The first romantic thing Chris did was subscribe me to the *St. Louis Post-Dispatch*. He liked to have his delivered and hoped I would, too. I pulled the newspaper out of its plastic wrapper and shuffled past the first few sections. There it was, in black and white, the story I pitched again and again until they finally took the bait. My hands were trembling with anticipation as I began to read.

The King's Castle: Graceland in Memphis, Tennessee
Views from a friend and a fanatic

"Elvis would have hated it." So says one of his best friends of what

the long-dead King of Rock 'n Roll would think about his Graceland home in Memphis today, which has become the second-most visited residence in the United States.

George Klein, now 71, is diminutive in stature but as a member of Elvis Presley's Memphis Mafia, his words carry weight. "Elvis was a very private guy," said Klein in a behind-the-scenes Graceland interview recently granted to this newspaper. "He really valued his time away from the limelight. Graceland was his sanctuary and I think he would be horrified to see it as a public space." Klein made these comments from the VIP Room, located in the mansion annex, sitting at the desk that was a gift to the King from RCA Records after the success of the Blue Hawaii movie soundtrack.

Horrified, maybe, but try telling that to 600,000 tourists who flock to the mansion annually. Maggie Coyle of St. Louis, a self-proclaimed Elvis fanatic born the day the King died—August 16, 1977—visits Graceland at least twice a year. "There are two types of people who go to Graceland," she said. "The first are typical tourists who are curious about Elvis, his home and his legacy. The second is a group whose lives have been affected by Elvis Presley—they're obsessed." Coyle identifies herself with the latter group. "My life was never the same after discovering this beautiful, talented man who captured hearts and changed music history."

How is it that one man, a poor kid from Tupelo, Mississippi, could amass such colossal, everlasting popularity? "He's the perfect combination," Coyle said. "Elvis had looks, charisma, talent and a mutual love affair with his fans." Of the guy he first met as an 8th grader at Humes High School in North Memphis in 1948, Klein said, "Elvis was an incredible entertainer, the biggest talent I've ever seen. He had an electricity and a voice that was magical."

Such electricity and magic that the man known worldwide by his first name has sold more records worldwide than any other artist, topping 1 billion and including gold, platinum and multi-platinum achievements. The total number of songs the King of Rock 'n Roll recorded is difficult to confirm, given his large amount of unreleased material, but multiple sources seem to agree on at least 700. More exact is that Elvis was nominated for 14 Grammys and won three for his gospel music. The National Academy of Recording Arts and Sciences also honored him with the Grammy Lifetime Achievement Award when he was just 36.

"Elvis was one of a kind, a living icon," Coyle said. "Women wanted him and men wanted to be him. Look at the Elvis Tribute Artist industry." The business of impersonating Elvis Presley grew in popularity after the King's death in 1977. All year long, Elvis festivals are held here in the U.S. and as far away as Australia and Japan, where professional Elvis tribute artists, or ETAs, entertain and compete in contests for the best representation of the legacy of Elvis Presley. Elvis Presley Enterprises recently announced the first-ever Ultimate Elvis Tribute Artist event, to be held this August during Elvis Week. EPE expects more than 20 of the best ETAs around the world to travel to Memphis to compete for this new designation.

300 miles to Graceland

From the St. Louis area, Graceland—the mecca for Elvis fans—is just under 300 miles away in the Whitehaven section of Memphis, straight down I-55 South. Elvis Presley Boulevard is the exit, thusly renamed from Highway 51 South in 1972.

In 1957, the 10,000-square-foot Colonial Revival mansion on 14 acres was empty and in need of repair. Graceland was built in 1939 by Dr. Thomas and Ruth Moore. Ruth named it after her Aunt Grace Toof, who inherited Graceland Farms from her father, S. C. Toof, a commercial printer in Memphis.

At 22, Elvis was living with his parents, Vernon and Gladys Presley, in a nice ranch home on Audubon Drive in Memphis, but fans were becoming a nuisance to the neighborhood. The young King, just coming into his stardom, gave his parents a $100,000 budget to look for something that would be more private.

Elvis bought Graceland on March 25, 1957 for $102,500. "He made a ton of improvements," Coyle said, rattling off details like only a true Elvis fanatic can do. "He built a stone wall around the property and *installed the signature musical gates. He put in a swimming pool and patio, racquetball court and the Meditation Garden." Elvis expanded the mansion, too. Today, the 18,000-square-foot home is a National Historic Landmark. Its most famous addition is the Jungle Room, where Elvis recorded his final two albums in 1976.*

A trip back in time

The Graceland tour allows a glimpse of the home as it was when Elvis was alive. For some, it's too gaudy—tacky even. For others, it's authentic to the 1970s and an eccentric King.

"Graceland may be frozen in history, but that's what's so great about it," Coyle said. "How many places can you go to today that are authentically preserved in time, as opposed to a recreation of the past? Americans are always tearing down something historic to replace it with something modern. Graceland is a real trip back in time," Laughing, she added, "I think the comments I receive most often after people tour the mansion are about the avocado-colored kitchen appliances. Anyone who grew up in the '70s remembers those."

Graceland is smaller than one would think, yet it's still a spectacle. Original furnishings and décor take visitors back to a time when Elvis walked the halls and lounged in its rooms. Colors abound, from stained glass peacocks in the living room to green shag Jungle Room carpet, from yellow lightning bolts on the basement wall to yards and yards of printed fabric on the ceiling above the pool table.

Upstairs is off limits, though. No one goes there except Priscilla, Lisa Marie and the curator, as Coyle pointed out. "Elvis died upstairs, so his private rooms remain that way, out of respect."

Coyle is surprised when she meets people who've never visited Graceland, especially when they're in St. Louis and it's just a few hours down the highway. "Of course, I immediately tell them to go," Coyle said. "It's a part of our history! Elvis was so very important to the 'possibility' of the music we listen to today. He did music his way and in doing so paved the path for a whole new sound, a whole new movement. Just ask anyone who was a teenager then. Graceland is where 'Elvis the artist' felt most free."

Klein added, "Graceland was Elvis' sanctuary. He really valued his time away from the limelight, surrounded by just family and close friends—people he could trust, people he could feel comfortable around." In addition to his parents, Elvis' group included his grandmother Minnie Mae Presley and rag-tag entourage of cousins, friends, bodyguards, valets and more who comprised the "Memphis Mafia."

Today, Elvis' only daughter, Lisa Marie Presley. owns Graceland and its possessions. CKX, Inc., an entertainment company with Priscilla Presley as one of its board members, manages the estate.

In addition to a tour of the Graceland mansion and grounds, tourists can see Elvis' car collection, airplanes and many other exhibits across Elvis Presley Boulevard.

While George Klein believes that Elvis would have hated seeing Graceland in its present state, he supposes it has a certain purpose. "Elvis loved his fans and they loved him, so I guess there's something good about this place that's dedicated to keeping his music and spirit alive."

Coyle agrees. "We must never forget Elvis Presley and his contributions to music and humanity. Graceland is the best way to share his impact with the world and spread it to future generations."

See for yourself. Your visit to Graceland begins at www.graceland.com.

"A trip back in time." Yes! Chris used my words. I was thrilled, vindicated even, and just now realized that I'd come back into the house and finished reading the article in my favorite chair.

I studied the photos. The newspaper used Chris' photo of George Klein at Elvis' desk in the VIP room. There were exterior photos of the front of Graceland, the musical gates and the Meditation Garden. I don't remember Chris taking those. The article also included interior photos of the stained-glass peacocks, the Jungle Room, a wall of Elvis' musical achievements in the Trophy Room and another in the former racquetball court. In a nice archival touch, there were two photos of Elvis and George from a Humes

High School yearbook.

I don't think Chris' story could have been any better. He created a true snapshot of Elvis, a real promo for his home and utilized the best from his interview with GK. Best of all, it set my heart pounding that I got to be the Elvis fan quoted in the story!

I looked around for my phone. As I called Chris, I glanced at the article again and noticed a sidebar in a gray box.

How to tell if you're an Elvis fanatic:

- *You collect every one of his 700+ songs and have more than one favorite.*
- *You can name all 31 of his movies plus 2 documentaries.*
- *You have a fully decorated "Elvis Room" in your home.*
- *You have scarves, leis and teddy bears from Elvis Tribute Artist concerts.*
- *Most of your vacation days are spent at Elvis festivals.*
- *You're a wind-up toy when it comes to Elvis trivia.*

Funny! And true. "Good morning, Sunshine," a voice interrupted my sidebar reading.

"Chris, it's great! I love it!" I exclaimed. "You did a superb job on the article."

"Well, good!" he replied.

"You captured Elvis, Graceland, the tour experience and your interview with George. I'm so excited!"

"I'm glad you like it."

"And the photos … I don't remember you taking those."

"I didn't, actually. Well, I took the one of George, but Elvis Presley Enterprises sent us the rest. They of course have better camera angles and lighting."

I laughed. "You should probably get a commission from EPE for future tour business!"

"I think that's called payola?"

"Whatever. You wrote a terrific teaser. And I love your 'trip back in time' angle!"

"I thought you would, my little time traveler," he teased. "Yeah, my editor was generous—1,300 words, 10 photos and a sidebar."

"The sidebar was funny! Could I possibly be the inspiration for it?" I laughed.

"Yes, you're quite the inspiration … more and more, it seems."

"Oh, really?" I loved this budding romance. "When do I get to inspire you in person?"

"How about dinner tonight?" he suggested.

"That would be perfect."

"OK. I'll pick you up around 7 p.m.?"

"Sounds good. You know where to find me." *Another date. Yes!*

It was Saturday and I was in a great mood. I did my usual weekend chores while walking on clouds. I worked out, took a nap and spent extra time picking out something to wear.

I listened to the evening news while I dolled up in skinny jeans, boots and a low-cut, figure-flattering sweater. I was blessed with a tall, thin frame, blue eyes and a smile that revealed straight, white teeth and two dimples. I could usually get by with just a touch of makeup. If I could change anything, it would be my curly hair. It took of most of my "get ready" time to tame what had a mind of its own. My current cut was an above-the-shoulders length with bangs.

When I was finally ready, I waited on the couch and noticed my journal on the end table. *Oh, Elvis.* My thoughts returned to the sexy King and I felt a little guilty for being such a two-timer. This wasn't fair to Chris but I didn't want to lose my connection with Elvis.

I took a couple of deep breaths and brought myself back to the moment. I have a date tonight, with a brown-eyed, handsome man and we seem to like each other. Let's see where it goes!

And we went there. *Whew!* I didn't plan for that to happen, not yet anyway, but we had a brewing passion for each other, like someone turned up the burner on a stove. Chris picked me up looking sharp in dark jeans and a button-down shirt. He smelled wonderful and I wanted to run my fingers through his dark, wavy hair.

We went to a local Italian place for dinner and realized we had our number one favorite food in common—pasta. We stuffed ourselves with salad, bread, olive oil and noodle dishes. We shared a bottle of wine and I started to unwind.

Chris was a good listener—a great trait for a reporter. I still had talking to do about my trip back in time. He let me go there. I was still processing the experience with Elvis Presley and wondering about the science that could make such a thing happen. I became emotional. Chris listened and comforted. At one point, he kissed my hand and said, "Let's get out of here."

The cold air snapped me out of my Elvis fog. Chris and I flirted all the way home. My wine buzz came in handy. I started that silly "red light" kissing game, making sure we kissed when we stopped at red lights. That only fueled the flames between us.

Once back at my house, we held hands on the way to the front door. As I put the key in the lock, I turned to him and said, "You're coming in, right?"

He answered with a kiss. We spilled into the entryway. Scatter came running up to greet me, then ran the other way when she saw Chris. I headed to the kitchen and turned on the light. Chris was right behind me. "Do you want some more wine?" I asked.

Again, his answer was a kiss, mixed with a, "Not really."

I kissed him back. "You wanna make out instead?"

"Uh-huh."

I flipped off the light. So many kisses. We were like teenagers with a newly discovered pastime. Coats came off and fell to the floor. Pressed against the refrigerator, I came up for air and said, "Let's go to the living room."

We sunk into the couch and slipped our shoes. I pulled Chris on top of me and we made out some more. It felt so good to have his weight on me. *I will not think about Elvis,* I silently promised myself.

Chris was gentle and sexy. Our hands started to wander. "Can we …" I started to ask, in between kissing and caressing.

"Can we what?"

"Go to the bedroom?"

He pushed himself up on his hands. Making eye contact, he asked, "Are you sure? We might reach the point of no return in there."

I playfully pushed him off of me. "I think we already have." I took him by the hand and led him to my bedroom. We shed the rest of our clothes, with the exception of underwear; I was suddenly shy. Chris reached into his wallet after he dropped his jeans to the floor. "I'm not going to charge you," I teased.

He produced a condom. "I come prepared."

That made me laugh. "No pun intended." We crawled under the covers. "Brrr! It's cold!"

"Come here and let me warm you up." He took me in to his arms and we were as close as we could be. "Maggie, we don't have to go any further," he said softly. "I really like you and don't want to mess anything up."

"I like you, too, Chris." My head was on his chest and I could feel his strong heartbeat. "This feels right, you and me. I know it's happening fast, but I care about you already and want to be with you." I looked up at him. We kissed. "I need you, Chris." *Make me forget about Elvis.*

Tangled together under the covers, I warmed up, and so did he. Underwear was kicked to the bottom of the bed. Naked and passionate, our hands roamed everywhere and so did our lips until it was time for two to become one. Chris ripped opened the little package and put the condom on so fast, it was impressive. We connected slowly, lovingly, beautifully. Boom. Fireworks for both of us, though not at the same time. I was taken away somewhere else, floating, relaxed.

"Very nice," he said quietly.

"I agree."

After lying together for a few minutes, side by side and hand in hand, Chris sat up and swung his legs over his side of the bed. "Um, Houston? We may have a problem."

"What's wrong?" He pointed to his groin area. I sat up and climbed over to take a look. "What happened? It looks like it's all rolled up at the end of your …"

"Yes, it does," he interrupted. "Yes, it is." He started rolling it forward so he could take the condom off.

"Did it break?"

"I guess so." He looked at me. "I'm sorry. This has never happened before."

At least he wore a condom. Elvis didn't. I could feel my heart pounding and wasn't sure if it was left over from sex or this plot twist. "That's OK. Well, it's not OK. Or maybe it will be OK," I stammered. "Actually, I think it is OK because of where I am in my monthly cycle." More determined. "Yes, it will be OK."

"Do you want me to leave?"

"No! I want you to stay … if you want to."

We took turns getting ready for bed in the bathroom. I offered him an extra toothbrush. We were both quiet, perhaps lost in thought. He held the covers open for me to crawl in. I noticed the cat was on the floor near the bed, wondering where she was going to fit in with the extra guest. I snuggled up next to Chris.

He kissed my forehead. "Sorry again about the …"

"Let's not talk about it," I interrupted.

He hugged me closer. "That was really fun tonight, Maggie. I hope you enjoyed it, too… even though I'm no Elvis."

Sigh. "No, you're not. Don't talk like that. You're Chris and you're here." I looked up at him. "We're together, and we've only just begun."

"Good night, Karen Carpenter."

That made me laugh. "And I did enjoy it, by the way. I hope we can do it again sometime."

"Give me an hour."

I groaned. "Good night, Chris."

I rolled away from him and we spooned. He fell right asleep. I envied him. It took me a while to slow the thoughts swirling in my head. *Chris, Elvis. Elvis, Chris. Both great guys. Chris is here, Elvis is not. Am I making a mess of things?*

CHAPTER 5

Mess of Blues

New Year's Eve, 1960

A search of the rest of the house and grounds did not turn up Maggie. When Red came through the front door, he found Elvis pacing up and down the front parlor. He had changed from his pajamas to navy blue pants and black boots, with a white leather zip-up jacket over a peach-colored button-down shirt with the collar up. He stopped when he saw Red. "She ain't here, is she?" he asked.

Red looked down, then back at Elvis. "No, boss, we can't find her anywhere. I'm sorry."

"Goddamnit!" Elvis shouted, and started pacing again. On his way back to where Red stood, he stopped and looked Red straight in the eye. "This is your fault. You never liked her and you made her go away. Why'd you do that, Red? It's none of your business who I wanna be with! And what's so terrible about Maggie in the first place?" There was fire in his eyes.

After the heated moment, Elvis said, "We're gonna take it into town." The King had formed another plan. "Fire up the Caddy," he directed Red. "I'm going with you." Then he brushed past him, leaving the room.

Red knew he needed to deescalate a fuming Elvis. "Elvis," Red called after him. "Why don't you let me take a drive and search around. It's gonna cause a scene if you're with me." He paused. "You know it will. I'll check out the places Maggie might have gone—the Peabody, Gerber's and such."

Elvis raised his hands to his forehead and Red envisioned another headache coming on. Softly, Red suggested, "Why don't you try to relax, and I'll report back to you as soon as I can. OK, boss?"

Elvis rubbed his eyes. When he looked at Red again, Red saw a bit of sadness mixed in with the anger. "Find her for me, Red. Please." With that, he turned and went up the stairs to his room.

"I will," Red replied, although he had no intention of bringing Maggie back to Graceland. "Hey, um, tonight is New Year's Eve. We're gonna have a great time."

Elvis paused on the landing, his hand on the doorknob to his bedroom door. He looked back down at Red. "Oh, yeah," he said, then chuckled. "I've got a date with Little." Little was his nickname for Anita Wood, the beautiful actress and singer from Memphis. They'd been pretty serious about each other for several years.

The phone was ringing when he walked in to his bedroom. He picked it up and Alberta said, "Miss Wood is on the line for you, Mr. Elvis."

Speak of the devil, he thought. "Thanks, VO5," he replied, then flopped across the bed to grab the receiver. "Hello?"

A dainty, sexy voice on the line said, "Hey, baby. How are you?"

"Hey, Little Bitty. I'm pissed off right now. We're dealing with a situation here."

"I'm sorry, honey. Do you want to talk about it?"

"No." A pause. "It's being taken care of."

"Well, that's good, because today is the last day of the year and tonight is New Year's Eve! I can't wait to see you. I miss you and I'm going to kiss you as many times as I can before the year is up!"

"Aw, I can't wait to get ahold of you!" Elvis groaned softly.

"Mmm, sounds like we're going to ring in 1961 just the way it should be."

"Yes, we will!" He flirted back.

"What time should I be ready? I've got a new dress, and I'm doing my hair and nails."

"I don't know. I'll ask one of the guys to give you a call and let you know. Sound good, baby girl?"

"Sounds great, my love. See you tonight!"

Hanging up the phone, Elvis remembered he'd told Maggie he had a date for New Year's Eve. He and Maggie had agreed to spend the couple of days and nights before December 31 together. "Time is short," she'd said to him. "Let's make the most of it."

"Sonofabitch!" he cursed, his flirty phone call forgotten. He started pacing again, his mind back on Maggie. He kicked at anything that was in his path. His foot stirred up an old newspaper. Sitting heavily on the edge of his big bed, Elvis pulled the paper off his boot and held it up to eye level. The top part was missing from the front page; it had been torn away. Suddenly, he remembered how it got like that. He'd written Maggie a note a couple of nights ago.

Elvis' anger was giving way to exasperation. "Aw, hell, Moody, where have you gone?"

CHAPTER 6

Starting Today

Happy New Year, 2007

I cherished the note that Elvis wrote to me on a piece of *Commercial Appeal* newsprint so much. It was proof—proof of my days and nights with Elvis, in his world, in December 1960. Here in my world, it was a New Year.

For the millionth time, I read the silly words he had scrawled. I didn't care that his penmanship resembled that of a serial killer.

M – misses her mama like I miss mine
O – pinions (O be quiet!)
O – oh so sexy
D – imples (also Different)
Y – ou're a stranger but you can see inside me
I can't figure her out but I like MOODY anyway.
Elvis

I loved my Moody nickname! I knew it was a sign that Elvis liked me. Most of the people he cared about had nicknames that he gave them, like Moon for Marty Lacker. I was a member of that special club.

I'd decided that Elvis' note to me was worth framing and had purchased a modest frame, something that looked nice and was portable in case I had to take it with me. Also, the glass would help preserve the piece from being touched a bunch of times.

It was displayed on the wall above my bedroom dresser. Elvis wrote the note in his bedroom, his words reflecting things we talked about and traits he recognized in me. Even though I'm smart enough to know our attraction was initially physical, I believe it became a deeper connection. Losing our mothers too soon broke our hearts. I understood Elvis because I came from a place in time where I'd had the opportunity to love him and learn about him. I think he knew that.

Chris, on the other hand, didn't see the squirrely love note the way I did, but it did make him curious. One evening, while we were lying in bed together after a luscious romp in the hay, he pointed to the framed note. "We should do some carbon dating on that thing."

"Carbon dating, ha!" I laughed at him. "Shall we send my Elvis note in with the Shroud of Turin and Dead Sea Scrolls?"

"It would answer a few questions," he said, remaining serious. I continued laughing. "If that note is from the past, and you traveled with it through some wrinkle in time, we could retire on the story we have to tell."

"Ooohh, now it's 'we,'" I teased him. "That means you believe me!" I'd been hoping he would believe my Elvis adventure really happened.

"Let's put it this way," Chris clarified. "I'll believe it when I see it."

That earned him an eye roll and a sigh. "I guess we're back to square one."

He rolled over on his side, facing me. "Square one, huh?" He kissed me. "This doesn't exactly seem like square one to me."

I rolled on my side, facing him. We were eye to eye, lips to lips. "You're right. I think we passed squares two and three, maybe even four? If you consider this a home run," I flirted back.

"I've definitely hit a home run. Meeting a girl like you—pretty, fun, smart. And single!" He entwined his fingers with mine. "I think I'm falling in love with you, Maggie Coyle."

"Chris Streater!" I feigned surprise. "Did you just say the L-word?"

"I said *an* L-word," he replied. "Not *the* L-word."

"Ah, I see."

"Is it a bad thing, that I said that?" He was suddenly insecure.

"Falling in love is never a bad thing!" I assured him. "It's wonderful, and something else we have in common."

"So, you're saying …"

"I'm saying that I'm falling in love with you, too." I completed his thought. "Correct that to past tense."

"You fell in love with me?"

"Yep."

"Wow."

"Wow is right." A pause. "I love you, Chris."

He broke into a big grin. "I love you, Maggie." He rolled on to his back and let out a big sigh. "I'm glad we got that straight."

"Me, too." I put my head on his shoulder, getting comfortable in the nook of his arm. "No pun intended."

"Too late."

CHAPTER 7

Baby, What You Want Me to Do

February 2007

I'd been feeling run down in the weeks following my return from Graceland. I attributed it to the stress and emotions, memories and lack of sleep. Chris and I were in love and getting more serious. Elvis was still on my mind.

As the days passed, my mental and physical health didn't improve. I was feeling like crap every morning and wishing I could take a nap every afternoon. Then it happened—or didn't, I should say. My monthly visitor was late, more than just a day or two. I ran to the drug store and bought a pregnancy test.

Women who've done this will understand when I say those five minutes between peeing on a stick and waiting for the plus or minus sign are agonizing. Uncertainty before certainty. Angst before joy, or sadness or relief.

I had set the timer on my phone and even though I knew it was coming, I jumped when it went off. My heart was pounding. Could I be pregnant? And if I am, when did I conceive? *God!* This could mean I actually don't know who the father is, something I never imagined for myself. I had tried to be a good girl, do the right thing and practice monogamy.

According to the over-the-counter test, I was pregnant. *Holy shit.* Well, that explains how I've been feeling lately. And it opens up a can of worms. As if my life was complicated enough with time travel and a new boyfriend!

I dropped to the couch. What I need is a level head. First thing I need to do is make a doctor appointment and find out for sure. No need to put the cart before the horse. I hope Chris won't pick up on this!

I'll be calm and logical. The answers will come. But what about the question that began its silent plague upon my heart: *Could this be Elvis Presley's child?*

It didn't take long to get a doctor appointment when I thought I might be pregnant; they got me right in. Two tests and one gyno exam later, I was told I'm going to have a baby. My doctor and nurse were positive and enthusiastic. I, on the other hand, wasn't sure how to react. I responded with a mix of laughter and tears.

Dr. Rightnour predicted my due date to be around September 21, 2007. I wasn't super helpful in getting to an exact date because I was wrestling with whether it was a result of fooling around with Elvis or with Chris. Despite the difference in decades, they were oddly just a few days apart. When the doctor asked the date of my last period, I guessed. I wasn't ready to deal with the paternity issue.

I was healthy and they expected me to have a normal pregnancy. That was good news. I was also young, so the doctor said she didn't anticipate any problems. Ha! Problems I seemed to have, as in figuring out when I'm going to tell Chris, and *if* I'll ever get to tell Elvis.

I can't stop thinking about him—Elvis—and I'm in love with Chris, which makes me a terrible person. A terrible *pregnant* person.

These thoughts consumed me the next several days. Going to work, working and coming home were robotic. I barely noticed my activities or the passage of time. Was this pregnancy brain? I felt a little crazy but tried to remain as normal as possible for Chris. He's a great guy and didn't deserve what was happening, or what he was about to find out.

I went back and forth in my mind, weighing pros and cons. I felt strongly that I couldn't let my pregnancy get in the way of finding out *if* I could go back and see Elvis again. And if I could, what would happen if I went back and could not return? My baby would be born in the 1960s!

Driving home one evening in cold February weather, I made two decisions. First, I was going to try to go back to Graceland and Elvis before the baby comes. Second, I was not going to tell Chris that I'm pregnant until after that.

When I got home, Chris had come over to make dinner. What a sweetheart—and not a bad cook. He had made something in the slow cooker: summer sausage, broccoli, brown rice and lots of cheese. A few minutes into our yummy meal, I decided to bring up the subject of returning to Memphis.

"I made a decision," I began emphatically.

"Oh yeah, about what?" he asked.

"I want to go back to Memphis, back to the hotel and try to go back to Graceland." Pause. "As soon as possible."

"Maggie, what's the rush? I told you I'd go with you, but it's the dead of winter and we were just there. Could we wait until spring when it would be more fun?"

"No." He didn't realize that this wasn't a negotiation. "I want to go now."

"Why?"

I took a breath. "Because I can't get it out of my mind. It's plaguing my thoughts! I must know if my time with Elvis was real. I have to prove it."

"To me? You don't need to prove anything to me, Maggie."

"To myself. I have to know, Chris."

"You just have to see *him* again." He fell quiet. We ate in silence. I looked at this sweet man who, like me, is in a new relationship. He's giving it his all, being romantic and a great friend. It pained me to think how much harder I could be trying.

"Chris," I began. "I don't expect you to understand. I know the whole thing is bonkers. You don't have to go. I just want to try. I want to get it over with, so I can give all of my attention to you, and us."

He remained quiet. I touched his hand. "Chris? What are you thinking?"

"I'm thinking that I'm in the twilight zone." I let him continue. "I met this girl whom I care about and love. I want to see what's going to happen, what kind of couple we could be." He paused. "But I'm in competition with Elvis Presley! Not the dead guy but apparently one who's alive and well in another time warp."

"I'm sorry," I said. "I really am. I know it doesn't make sense. I care about you and love you, too. Right now, all I'm asking for is your support."

He considered it. "I suppose that supporting you includes the twilight zone, so you have it." He squeezed my hand. "Let's bang our calendars together and see when we can hit the road."

"Thank you!" I jumped up from my chair to hug and kiss him. "Thank you so much!"

"Don't you mean 'thank you, thank you very much'?" he responded, with an Elvis intonation.

"Everyone's an Elvis impersonator!"

Chris spent the night. After the dinner dishes, I changed into pajamas and immediately started planning our trip.

"It's February 2007," I said, more to myself than anyone else. "If I can get back to Elvis similarly to last time, it could be February 1961. What's he up to?"

"Getting laid whenever he wants," Chris said.

"Ha! Look who's talking." I reached for my favorite Elvis encyclopedia on the book shelf and looked up the King's 1961 highlights. "This must be meant to be! He's at Graceland this month!"

"How convenient."

"Sarcasm?" I asked, then moved on. "On February 25, the Governor will declare it Elvis Presley Day in Memphis and Elvis will mark the occasion by raising money for charity." I look at Chris for emphasis. "He was *such* a generous guy."

"Good for him." Chris sounded unimpressed.

"In March and April of 1961, he'll be filming *Blue Hawaii,* starting in Hawaii and finishing in California." I looked at Chris again. "If I'm going to try to get back to him, we need to go now."

"How about right after another mattress mambo?"

"Well, of course!" I replied, realizing it was time to pay attention to my boyfriend.

That night, snuggled up to the sound of Chris' breathing beside me, I thanked my lucky stars to have a man who's supportive of my quest to prove that my "waking up in Graceland" was legitimate. He may just be humoring me, but I'm grateful to have someone who will help me and wait for me to come back.

That said, there's *no way* he'd let me do this if he knew I was pregnant.

CHAPTER 8

Hard-Headed Woman

February 16, 2007

Neither Chris nor I had weekend plans, so we decided to hit the road late Friday afternoon. I had a rough start to the day with morning sickness. All I could stomach was white soda and crackers, and the car ride didn't help. Chris was sweet; he drove the whole way. I told him I had a headache and some car sickness.

We were relatively quiet. I recalled the opposite experience from the first time we drove to Memphis together for his story assignment. We had played "20 Questions." He learned a lot about Elvis for his article while I learned a lot about him; for example, how he grew up in Chicago, was married before and wanted to write a screenplay some day.

Out of the silence, we spoke at the same time. He said, "We had two hotel rooms last time," as I blurted, "Have you started on your screenplay project?"

We both laughed at the clashing conversation. "What did you say about two hotel rooms?" I asked.

"I was just thinking how times have changed. Last trip to Memphis, we needed two hotel rooms. This time, we just need one."

"Ah, true. That's because I have to keep my eye on you."

"What?" He feigned surprise. "You don't trust me?"

"No. I completely trust you. I just want to keep my eye on you because you're such a hunk."

"Oh, I see." He laughed. "A hunka hunka burnin' love?" he asked, trying his best to sound like Elvis.

I laughed, too. "Kind of, yes."

"And what did you say about my screenplay?"

"I was just wondering if you ever started writing one."

"Not yet. But soon, I think. No more excuses! I've got to make the time."

"What's your movie going to be about?"

"I'm not sure yet. Maybe time travel? A girl who thinks she can go back through a magic portal to Elvis Presley."

"Very funny," I replied.

"Well, it's something to think about. Could be a good story. But I have some other ideas brewing, too."

"I bet you do." With that, we both got lost in our own thoughts again. I was tired and my stomach was still doing flip flops. With the purring of the engine, I drifted off to a nap.

"Maggie." A voice called my name from somewhere. "Hey lover," it said again. I felt a warm hand on mine. I opened my eyes, groggy about my surroundings. "Your favorite highway exit is coming up," Chris said. My brain rejoined reality and I saw that we were getting closer to Graceland.

"Ah, Elvis Presley Boulevard. Yay!" I responded. "How long was I asleep?" I felt better.

"You were out of it," Chris said, squeezing my hand. "I guess you needed the rest." He paused. "You've been tired a lot Maggie … is everything OK?" He looked over at me. "When was the last time you had a checkup?"

I was quiet for a moment. I hated being untruthful, but he can't learn that I'm pregnant or he'll never let me attempt another trip back in time. "I'm fine." I squeezed his hand back. "No worries. Just needed some Zs. Thanks for driving and getting us here safely."

"And here it is—the road to Graceland!" Chris exclaimed for my benefit.

I sat up in my seat and shook off some cobwebs. The realization of why we were here, and what I was about to do, settled back in.

"Chris," I began. "We're really going to do this, right?"

"Correction: you're going to do it and I'm going to watch," he answered, then laughed. "Hey that sounds kinda hot. What do you say we get a *little* crazy before you do something *totally* crazy?"

I looked at him, forgetting his sexual pun. "You think I'm crazy."

"No, I don't. But c'mon. We just drove 300 miles to see if you can get back to the 1960s. You gotta admit—it's a bit nutso."

I sighed. "It does." I glanced longingly at the gates leading up to Graceland as we drove past, heading to the hotel up ahead. "But we've talked about this and you know I have to try or I won't be able to live with myself. I have to know that my time with Elvis was real. I have to see him again, if possible."

"I know. I may be Chris Streater, sexy newspaperman and boyfriend extraordinaire, but I'm not Elvis Presley. I'll just settle for sloppy seconds," he said, giving me a puppy dog look.

"What you are is wonderful and supportive. What I've asked you to do is not normal, I know. Thanks, honey, for being you. I love you."

Chris pulled the car into the Days Inn Graceland parking lot. "Awesome. Let's get a room and get naked."

Check-in went smoothly. I was able to reserve the same room as before. I told them it was our anniversary and the room had special meaning. It was a cute hotel with Elvis-themed décor. The lobby was full of framed photos on the wall, statues and more.

Chris had his hands full with our travel bags so I let us in to Room 222. My eyes immediately went to the wall on the other side of the king size bed. Could it be? My mind raced through the thoughts I'd had since waking up in Graceland. Did other guests who slept in that bed turn up in Graceland 1960? How could maids change the bed without falling through?

Chris set our bags on the dresser, tossed his keys on the nightstand and flopped down on the other bed. He reached for me. "C'mere, beautiful. Let me hold you after a long drive."

I acquiesced. I was gung-ho to try the time traveling thing again, but I was in a relationship, too, and relationships mean compromise. Chris traveled here with me to provide support, even though he didn't really believe anything was going to happen. I loved him for that—I loved him for a lot of reasons. We'd come a long way in a couple of months. He didn't need to twist my arm. We made love right there in Room 222, and we were good at it.

After our quality time, I got right back to the task at hand. "OK," I said, emphatically. "We're going to try this sooner than later. I'm going to get changed ..."

"Into something more 1960s?" Chris finished my sentence.

"Precisely." I got out of bed and grabbed my duffle bag.

Chris laid on his side, propping his head up on his hand. He stared at the other bed. "So that bed is actually a time machine?" He stifled a laugh, which made me feel self-conscious.

I gave him a look. Doubt was creeping in. "We're about to find out." I went to the bathroom to change and freshen up. I'd done my homework and found an outfit that looked like a 1960s throwback: brown stretch pants with seams running down the center of each leg, a brown and white horizontal stripe long-sleeve turtleneck sweater and black ankle boots. I brushed my teeth and touched up my makeup. I packed a few cosmetics into my purse, which was all I planned to take with me.

When I came out of the bathroom, Chris was sitting on the edge of the bed, channel surfing. "OK, I'll give you 1960s with that look."

"Thanks." I put my other clothes on the dresser and stood between him and the TV. I took his face in my hands. "As Elvis would say, it's now or never. Let's give this time travel thing a try." I kissed him on the forehead. "And by the way, I love you." I kissed him on the lips.

His eyes held my gaze. "I love you, too. I guess I'm as ready as I'll ever be for my girl to disappear to chase after another man." I rolled my eyes at him. "Where do you want me?" he asked.

"Well, how about you stay on that side of the room and I'll get on this bed, move around a bit, and see what happens," I replied.

"OK." He grabbed the remote control and scooted back on the bed, sitting up against the pillows and headboard. I followed and kissed him again.

"Let's do this," I said, mustering determination when, quite honestly, my heart pounded at the possibility of what could happen. I looked at Chris one more time then crawled on top of the other bed. What passed through my mind again was that this bed had been flipped by the maids many times since I was last here. Was there a string of people who disappeared?

I moved around the bed, first the side closest to Chris, then the other. Nothing happened. I crawled to the head of the bed, then the foot. Still nothing. I couldn't look at Chris; I was starting to feel foolish. I sat in the center of the bed, cross legged, my back to him. Thinking. If it wasn't the bed I passed though, could it be the floor between the bed and the wall? Or the wall itself? I scooted up to the edge of the bed and looked down at the floor. It was a narrow space, and nothing seemed different or strange. I looked at the wall. Nothing out of the ordinary.

Feeling eyes in the back of my head, I turned around to look at Chris. He gave me an inquisitive look and shrugged his shoulders. "Nothing happening?" I could tell he was trying to be a good sport when he probably wanted to bust out laughing.

I was still determined to make this work. I crawled off the bed into the small floor space between it and the wall. Slowly, I paced forward and backward. I repeated that a few times. Nothing. I faced the wall and started running my hands all over it. I even took the Elvis wall hanging down and placed it on the bed. I roamed as far up and down as I could reach and nothing happened. Damn! This was frustrating and humiliating. I wasn't going anywhere in Room 222 after all. I would not see Elvis. I plopped down on the bed, defeated, and began to cry.

Chris joined me on the bed. "Maggie." His tone was soft,

consoling. "It's OK. Don't cry. Come here." He pulled me into his arms. I buried my face in his shirt.

"I'm so confused. I don't understand," I said through tears. "It was here. It was real. Oh, Elvis!" More tears.

Chris held me while I cried. Eventually, he spoke. "If I'm being honest, Maggie, I'm a little relieved." I looked up at him. "I mean, I've been feeling a little jealous about how anxious you've been to get back to Elvis. Like he's more important than I am."

I shook my head. "He's not, Chris. He's just … Elvis."

"I know, the King of Rock 'n Roll. Imagine how that feels. There's no way I can compete with Elvis, so I'm kind of glad you can't get back to Graceland." He pushed back some curls and kissed me on the forehead. "I guess your time portal took off on another adventure. But isn't *my* love enough for you, Maggie?"

Took off. That made me think. I wiggled out of his hug and sat up in bed. "That's it!"

"What?" Chris looked puzzled. "My love *is* enough for you to forget about seeing Elvis again?"

"No." I was on to something. "I mean, yes. Chris, I love you. You're my guy." I changed the subject. "You said maybe the time portal took off. What if that's exactly what it did? What if it moved somewhere else? It could be somewhere nearby!" I jumped off the bed and began a detailed search of the room.

"Maggie …" Chris shook his head. "Can't we just give up on this fantasy?"

"You can give up on this if you want. But I'm not going to." I was a little defiant. "It's not a fantasy! If I could get back to Graceland, it would be real, and a good thing. I need to see Elvis. I need to talk to him." I wasn't ready to tell Chris exactly why, so I fabricated. "I think I can help him. And maybe he won't have to die so young."

Chris breathed a heavy sigh. Admittedly, I felt bad for him, putting up with a nutcase like me. I understood that he didn't have to, and could choose to leave me if he didn't think our relationship was worth it.

"Hey," I went over to him on the bed, where he was picking up the remote. I kissed him on the mouth. "I'm so grateful for you. You've been a big support to me. I understand if you think this time travel stuff is whacked out, but until I hit a brick wall, I have to try." I took his hand in mine. "What do you say I spend some time searching—the room, maybe the hallways—and if I don't disappear, we'll go and make some memories on Beale Street?" I hadn't yet figure out how I was going to *not* drink.

"Sounds like a plan," he replied. "And could you hurry up? I'm hungry."

I rolled my eyes. "Sex and food. That's really all you men think about!"

"Right. And that includes Elvis, so remember that."

Chris relaxed on the bed watching TV while I conducted a thorough search of Room 222. I was taking it seriously; he was not. When I bent over to look extra hard for a mysterious portal behind pieces of furniture, he'd start laughing. Eventually, I joined in, too. It *was* ridiculous, what I was doing, but I had to be sure. No one but me knew why I wanted to see Elvis again.

I checked every wall, every inch of floor. I even used an untwisted hanger to reach under the beds and behind the headboards. When I got back in the spot where I fell through to 1960 three months ago, I jumped up and down, just to make sure there was nothing there.

"Stop laughing at me!" I said to him, then cracked up myself.

"Did you find anything?" Still laughing.

"Stop it. No."

"Let me know when you're hungry and we'll go get something to eat."

"Translation: *I'm* hungry. As in *you.*" I didn't want to admit that I was hungry, too, because I wasn't quite finished yet. "I'm going to check around outside, then we can head to Beale." I grabbed my coat and headed for the door. I turned around and his eyes were back on the screen. "Hey, if I don't come back in the next 15 minutes, send out a search party?"

He looked at me. "Of course. I'll conduct the search myself."

"Just remember, you might have to come looking for me in the 1960s." I didn't wait for his response; I left the room and closed the door behind me.

Outside, I walked slowly up and down the exterior hallway, using hands and fingers, feet and toes to feel into the corners and cracks. How far does a time portal move? I had no idea. Should I search other floors? Do I look like a freak? If someone stopped me, I could say I lost a contact lens or piece of jewelry.

With each step, my discouragement grew. In a way, I was getting the answer I sought: the portal was not here anymore. *Get on with your life, girl. You have a good man and you're going to have his child.* On the flip side, my burning questions were still unanswered: Was my time with Elvis real? Will I ever see him again? Am I carrying his baby?

I must have looked forlorn. In the third floor exterior hallway, a maid stopped me. "Is everything alright, miss? Do you need any help?"

"I'm OK, I'm, uh, just looking for something I lost."

"I'm sorry, dear. If you tell me what it is, I'll help you look."

"Thanks. It's kind of hard to describe." Forgetting to lie about a contact lens or jewelry, I continued. "It's a pathway to somewhere else—from here to there, a way out."

She cocked her head and looked at me sideways. "Way out, uh huh, OK. Well, I'll keep my eyes open and you be sure to call the front desk if we can make your stay more comfortable." Under her breath, she added, "Or if you need help finding your room."

She thought I was lost, or losing my mind. Maybe I was. "Thank you," was my only response.

When I let myself into our room, Chris blurted out, "I'm huuuuungry!"

"Alright, alright!" I replied. "I give up. Let's go."

He saw the disappointment on my face and scooted off the bed to put his arms around me. "Aw, babe, I'm sorry. You didn't find the portal anywhere outside this room?"

"No, I didn't. I guess it's … gone." Being held in his arms made me feel better. "I'm disappointed, I'm sad, but what else can I do?"

He kissed me. "I'm sorry," he said again. "I love you. Maybe we can just make this about the two of us now? No more love triangle with Elvis Presley?"

"Yes." I kissed him back. "I love you, too." I hugged him tighter. "I still love Elvis, but I guess the past is in the past."

"That it is. And dinner and drinks are in the future!"

As we left the hotel and headed downtown, I thought about how it really wouldn't be "just the two of us" as Chris suggested. I would never be able to totally let go of Elvis. And there was another *person* on the way.

We decided on Blues City Café for dinner, at the top of Beale Street. They had delicious barbecue and catfish. Chris ordered a half rack of ribs and I had the catfish. When he ordered a couple of beers for us, I jumped in. "Not for me right now. You go ahead. I think I'll wait." This generated a curious look from him. I didn't often turn down a beer, but Chris didn't make a deal out of it.

We ate until we were stuffed. He had two or three beers—I wasn't counting. Dessert sounded good to me so we split a slice of pecan pie with ice cream.

After dinner, we headed down Beale on foot. Even though it was cold, we could still hear the music pulsing from inside each bar. Such a variety—blues, hip hop, pop and R&B. We walked faster than we would in warmer weather, and soon chose Mr. Handy's Blues Hall to go inside. Over the noise, Chris said, "Let's do a shot! What do you want?"

"I don't want a shot," I replied loudly.

"Why not?"

"I'm not in the mood for one."

He put his arm around me and rubbed my back. "Everything OK? If you're tired or something, we can go back to the room."

"I'm fine. And I like the music. Let's stay for a while. You can do as many shots as you want. I'll be your designated driver."

"Sweet!" He bellied up to the bar and ordered a Purple Hooter. When the bartender handed it to him, he raised the glass and saluted me. "For old time's sake."

We had shot Purple Hooters on our last trip to Memphis at Coyote Ugly. "Cheers to us," I replied.

We hung out at the Blues Hall for a while, then braved the cold for a short walk to our next stop, Silky O'Sullivan's. By now, Chris was feeling pretty good. He made a beeline for the bar and I followed. When we got there, he said, "Do you wanna do a shot with me now? Or a beer?"

"Still not."

"Alright!" He turned away from me and ordered a shot of tequila. Blech. The thought of that on top of Purple Hooter made my stomach turn.

After Chris followed his tequila with salt and lime, we found a nook to listen to the live music. He leaned against the wall and pulled me in front of him, wrapping his arms around me. Admittedly, I was comforted. He kissed me a few times on the neck, which sent shivers down my spine.

"I'm feeling pretty good right now, Maggie. I wish you were, too."

"I feel fine. I just don't feel like drinking."

"It's not like you."

"I know, but I have my reasons."

He spun me around to face him and kissed me. Now we looked like a lovesick couple making out in the corner. "What possible reason could you have not to have a few drinks in downtown Memphis?"

I kissed him back. I looked him in the eye. *Here goes.* "I'm pregnant."

Chris busted out laughing. "Ha! Good one! You got me there. Pregnant. Ha!"

I wasn't laughing. I remained silent, keeping eye contact. The music blared. His expression changed, perhaps a shot of sobriety. "Holy crap. Are you serious? You're pregnant?"

I blinked my eyes in agreement, nodded my head slightly. "Yes. I am."

He pushed me away a bit, absorbing the bombshell I just dropped. "You're going to have my baby?"

Do I go there now? After a moment, I replied with a half-smile, "I think so."

He dropped his arms to his sides. "You think so. What, you're not sure it's mine?"

"Chris." I took each of his hands in mine. "I didn't mean to tell you this way. It's too … loud in here. Can we leave and go someplace quieter to talk?"

He shrugged. "Sure. Yeah. Let's get out of here." As we headed toward the door, he added, "Major buzz kill."

Outside Silky's, we zipped up our coats and put on gloves. Chris put on his hat. He was quiet. Instead of what I thought he would do, head farther down Beale Street, he took my hand and led me up the street, in the direction of where we parked.

"We don't have to leave," I offered. "We can hang out and listen to more music."

"Nah," he replied. "Let's go back to the hotel where it's warm. And quiet." He hiccupped. "You're driving."

"Of course." After a moment, "I'm sorry I killed your buzz."

"No matter," he shrugged. "It wasn't going to last forever."

We reached our parking space in the garage in silence. He handed me the keys and I got in on the driver's side. He climbed into the passenger seat. I drove us out of the garage, out of downtown Memphis and on to the highway for the short ride to Elvis Presley Boulevard and our hotel.

I was about to say something to break the silence when Chris suddenly slammed his gloved hand on the dashboard. It made me jump. "You know, the more I think about it, Maggie, the madder I get! You're pregnant, and you were going to time travel! What is going on in that head of yours?"

Calmly, I replied. "I can explain."

"Ha!" he bellowed. "Explain away. Please."

"Could you bring it down a notch, maybe? I'm pregnant, after all. I shouldn't get upset."

"Pregnant. Oh my God. This is major."

"Yes, it is. And I'm sorry you found out in a bar. I didn't plan it that way—you just wouldn't let up on me not drinking."

"I couldn't think of a reason why you wouldn't!" Exasperation. "Gosh, this could be big, exciting news for us, yet you go and do things that make no sense."

"You know as well as I do that I had to know if I could go back through the portal to Elvis—pregnant or not."

"Elvis, Elvis, Elvis. Didn't you just say, before dinner, no more love triangle?"

"No, you said that. I said, 'the past is in the past.'"

"Right! If the past is in the past, why can't we leave it there?"

"Well, it pretty much is! I didn't find my way back, did I?"

"No. But you knew you were pregnant and you tried anyway. That's even crazier than the trying part! You're going to have a baby and you're not thinking about what's safe!"

"You're right. I'm sorry," I said as I pulled the car into the hotel parking lot. "But I've been thinking about it. A lot. I've been overwhelmed and obsessing over what has happened and what I should do."

I pulled into a parking space and kept the engine running. Chris started shaking his head. "What? You don't want me to park here?"

"Damn." He held his head in his hands and spoke. "My head is spinning. My girlfriend told me she's pregnant, and every time I start to get excited about it, I remember that she said, 'I think so,' which makes me wanna puke."

"A spinning head and wanting to puke sounds more to me like the result of your overindulging tonight."

"Whatever." He looked at me with hurt in his eyes. "When I asked you if you were going to have my baby, why did you say, 'I think so'?"

I turned a bit to face him. "If I'm being honest with you, I had sex with you *and* Elvis Presley within a matter of days. So, technically, I don't exactly know who the father is, and I'm sorry about that."

Another hand slamming into the dash. "This is ludicrous, Maggie! I know you're convinced your time with Elvis really happened, but we just tried to prove it and it failed!"

"But …"

"No buts! When are you going to let all of this time travel/Elvis Presley stuff go?"

"First of all, calm down. And have you forgotten about the note he left me … on 1960 newspaper? What about that? You said we need to get it carbon dated. Doesn't the note at least raise the question that I might be telling the truth?"

"Gah!" he exclaimed. "You're frustrating the hell out of me!"

I turned off the car. "It's cold. Let's go inside." I got out. He trailed behind me to the room. When we entered, I cranked up the heat. Chris flopped on the bed. I wanted to resolve this conversation but was ready for my pajamas. I quietly undressed and prepared for bed. Chris fidgeted with the remote in his hands but didn't turn the TV on.

Me being pregnant was major news; however, I couldn't decide if we should keep talking about it. I pulled back the covers of the bed Chris was lying on and climbed in. I curled up on my side, facing him, and reached for his hand. He pulled away, but thankfully only to stand up, shed a few pieces of clothing, pull back the covers on his side of the bed and climb in next to me, facing me.

We stared into each other's eyes, our minds and hearts swirling with thoughts and emotions. I broke the silence. “I’m sorry about tonight. Yes, I’m pregnant. I’m going to have a baby. I’m going to take good care of myself, and this child. I love you and hope we can have this experience together.”

He reached under the covers and put his hand on my stomach. “I love you, too. But you’re kind of breaking my heart, Maggie.” He stroked my stomach. “Is this Baby Streater, or Baby Presley?”

I kissed him on the nose. Under the covers, I rested my hand on top of his. “For now, my love, this is Baby Coyle.” I snuggled in to him. The lights were still on, but I fell fast asleep.

The next day, we headed back to St. Louis. I was tired and defeated. There wasn’t a good enough reason to stay another night. We had deep talks on the way home, and made a big decision—he was going to move in. We were going to live together!

Chris considered himself the father of this baby. I sort of hoped he was right.

CHAPTER 9

Help Me

Three months later

Pregnancy made me loony. About halfway through, I decided it wasn't a good idea to give up on trying to get back to Elvis. My thinking was, if I figured out how to get there, I could come back like I did last time. What was the harm? I had plenty of time to have a baby in the present.

Chris had lost interest after I failed to find the portal and was still testy about the fact that I tried to go back while pregnant. I think I convinced him that I was completely focused on my pregnancy and wouldn't do anything risky.

Behind the scenes, my time with Elvis pulled at me like a magnet. My hormones were raging; I was on an emotional roller coaster. When I thought about him, it was like my heart was being tugged out of my chest—toward him, as if we were connected across space and time.

I needed help and knew just who to enlist: my siblings. Each of them had obsessions that I could use as bait to convince them to help me with my next attempt. For my brother, it was time travel. For my sister, it was fashion.

I'm the oldest of three: Joan Magdalene Coyle (that's me), Mark Joshua and Sarah Jennifer. We grew up with a normal, middle-class existence; we didn't want for anything. Dad worked, Mom stayed home and we went to Catholic school. My parents made birthdays and holidays special and memorable. We had a nice home, with plenty of clothes, food and toys.

My brother Mark is one of a kind. Tall, nice looking, blue eyes. He got the curly hair like I did, so he wore it pretty tight with plenty of gel. He was born three years after me, my parents' only son. Mom used to tell me how I'd imitate her caring for my baby brother with my baby doll.

Mark is smart and well-versed in a lot of subjects: foreign languages, classical music, heavy metal music, horror movies and science fiction. Sometimes, though, I wonder if he has common sense. He does nutty things, like having two serious girlfriends at once. He'll take one on a date and crash at her place. He'll take the other one out and have her spend the night with him. How does he do it?

Mark drives his car without a seat belt and rides his motorcycle without a helmet. He may be able to say "helmet" in four languages but doesn't think about the head injury he'd suffer if he got in an accident.

When it comes to my other sibling, the first thing I remember *wanting* as a kid was a sister. I wanted a little girl to play with, love, nurture, dress up and show off to my friends.

When Mom told us she was pregnant again, I was 6 and over the moon! I told my teachers that Mom was having a girl. How did I know? I prayed every day for a baby sister.

Sarah was born in 1984. She was everything I dreamed of and more: cute, smiley, silly and as far as I was concerned, mine. She followed me everywhere. I was always dressing her up and doing her hair; she actually seemed to care about what she was wearing and how she looked.

Sarah's passion for fashion carried through her teen years and into adulthood. With an emphasis on vintage items from the 1960s, she put thought and purpose behind each of her ensembles. She was a beauty—a bit taller than me, thin, blue eyes and, lucky her, *long straight hair.* Heads turned when she walked into a room.

I love my siblings, and when they find out what happened to me in Memphis, I think they'll be champions for my cause to get back to Elvis. Mark's curiosity will get the better of him and Sarah will flip if she gets the chance to see her favorite clothing in its original time.

I decided to call a "family meeting," inviting them over one evening after work. The only thing I told them to get them there was that Dad was not invited. Maybe they thought something was wrong with him, or even with me and the baby, so they were both responsive and got to my place as soon as they could.

Sarah arrived first with a bottle of wine. "I know you can't have any, but I need some," she said as I let her in. "What's going on? Are you OK? Is Dad OK? What's wrong, sis?"

"Don't worry, stop freaking out. Everything is OK," I reassured her, taking the bottle from her and heading to the kitchen. Sarah followed me. "I just need to confide in both of you about something." I opened the cabinet to retrieve a wine glass and placed it on the counter. "And I need your help."

She gave me her exasperated look. "Is that supposed to make me feel better? Now you have some big secret I don't know about?"

"Calm down, please. I actually think what I'm going to tell you will interest you." I handed her the wine opener; I was inept at opening bottles of wine.

That piqued her curiosity. "Fine. Care to give me a sneak preview before Mark gets here?"

Shaking her head at me, she opened the bottle and poured herself a glass. I poured a glass of sparkling water.

We sat on the couch in the living room, killing time. She was telling me the latest story about her annoying boss at work when Mark knocked on the door and let himself in. "Don't say a word," he said, passing through to the kitchen, "until I have a beer in my hand." My brother knew I would have beer in the fridge, even though I was on a hiatus from drinking.

"Hello to you, too, brother," Sarah called after him.

"Hey, Mark, make yourself at home. Beer's in the fridge," I added, laughing at him.

Mark twisted off the cap and snapped it across the room, which meant I would find it next time I cleaned the house. "Oh, yeah, hi sisters. And thanks, Mags, for the brewski." He took a big swig and sat down in the chair across from the couch. "What the hell is going on? Spill it."

"Both of you are so dramatic!" I exclaimed. "What makes you think I have something shocking or scary to say?"

"Because you called a 'family meeting.' Duh," Mark replied.

"I needed to talk to both of you together and that seemed like the best way to get you here as quickly as possible," I said. "I'm sorry if I worried you."

"She has a secret," Sarah told Mark, swirling the wine in her glass.

"Oooh, do tell!" Now he was interested.

"OK, you two," I began. "Promise me you'll listen to what I have to say and save your questions for when I'm finished."

Mark and Sarah exchanged looks and nodded their consent.

"Remember when I took Chris to Memphis to write a story about Elvis and Graceland?" They nodded again. "Well, that was a bigger experience than I ever told you."

Mark laughed. "Yeah, because you got a boyfriend and he knocked you up." Sarah giggled.

I decided to forge ahead. "Yes, you're right. But only partially because what I haven't told you yet is even more powerful." Now I had their full attention. "After Chris and I toured Graceland, and after partying on Beale Street, something happened in my hotel room."

Mark rolled his eyes. "Seriously. You don't need to paint this picture." He took a long drink of his beer.

"Yes, I do. Chris went back to his room. I was alone. I'd had too much to drink and passed out on the bed …"

Sarah shifted in her seat. "If he attacked you while you were drunk, I swear I'll kick his …"

"Sarah!" I interrupted. "Don't jump to conclusions! Just listen." I paused, regaining my story line. "I went somewhere else. Not a dream. When I woke up, I was in a different place. I wasn't in my hotel room … I was … at Graceland."

For once, they were quiet. I made eye contact with each of them before continuing. "I was in a closet in the basement and soon learned that the time had changed. It wasn't 2006. It was 1960."

They looked at each other, then back at me. I made another attempt at clarity. "What I'm trying to say is that I went back in time. I met Elvis Presley. And spent a few days with him."

"What the … *hell,* Maggie? Have you lost it?" Mark blurted out.

Sarah added, "Are you sure it wasn't a dream?"

"It wasn't," I emphasized. "Mark, I know you love this stuff. You heard what I said, right? I traveled through time! And, Sarah, I wore 1960s clothing. Elvis sent me on a shopping spree you would have loved!"

"Maggie, time travel is not scientifically possible," Mark said. "You just had a crazy, alcohol-induced dream."

Sarah nodded in agreement. "You'd just spent the entire day talking about all things Elvis with a reporter, so the content was fresh in your mind."

I stood up; I had more convincing to do. "I can prove it happened. I can prove I traveled back to 1960 Graceland." Registering their surprised looks, I left the room to retrieve the evidence from my bedroom.

Mark and Sarah were still quiet when I returned with the frame, my MOODY note that Elvis had written me on a scrap of newspaper. "Let me begin my saying that what I'm about to show you really got Chris' attention when he first saw it. He didn't want to believe me at first, just like you two. We were in the car on our way back from Memphis and I found this note wrapped around my Elvis sunglasses. Which, by the way, had traveled to the past with me and back to the present." I held out the frame so they both could see. Sarah took in into her hands. Mark left his chair and joined her on the couch.

"Elvis wrote this to me. Moody was his nickname for me. You can see what he wrote it on. It's from the Memphis newspaper, the top part of the front page. With the date. Look at the date," I persuaded. "What does it say, Mark?"

"The *Commercial Appeal.* December 29…" Mark read.

"1960!" Sarah finished. After a moment, she added, "Maggie, if this is some kind of a joke, please stop now."

Mark got quiet, which could be a good sign. "The fact that Elvis Presley wrote a note on a scrap of 1960 newsprint to a girl named Moody doesn't prove that you, my sister, traveled back in time."

I wasn't giving up. "Chris thought the note was freaky."

"On that we agree," Sarah said.

I continued. "Freaky enough to go back to Memphis with me and try again."

"Try again?" Mark asked.

"Yep. As soon as we could make plans to go back to the same hotel, same room, we went back to Memphis. He was great about it. Only …"

"Only what?" Sarah asked.

"Only it didn't work. I couldn't find the portal, or whatever you call it," I said, focusing on Mark. "The first time, it was somewhere between the hotel bed and the wall of Room 222. The second time, it just wasn't there." I paused. "I was so bummed. I even searched most of the rest of the hotel, what I could get to anyway, just in case it moved somehow. Chris was a really good sport, but after I couldn't show him how I time traveled, he gave up. He told me to give it up, too, that it just must have been one helluva dream."

"I'm inclined to agree with him," Sarah said, then added, "Sorry, sis." She handed the Moody frame back to me.

Holding the note Elvis wrote to me, I sighed. I closed my eyes, imagining him and me together, those precious moments we shared. That, combined with the fact that I was pregnant with Lord knows whose child, spurred me onward. I zeroed in on my brother, the science fiction geek. "Don't you want to know what it was like,

Mark? The time traveling part? I can describe it for you!"

Mark remained quiet. I changed focus to Sarah. "Sarah, I can tell you each and every outfit I bought on the shopping spree, what Elvis wore, what the other women wore, how they did their hair and makeup. I know how much you love that stuff!"

Despite my pleas for attention, they were both still quiet. "Look at me," I begged. They did. "Look at your big sis who's about halfway through a pregnancy. Because of what I went thru five months ago, not just with Chris but with what I believe to be a legitimate experience with Elvis Presley …" I decided to go for it. "We don't know who the father of this child is!" I was about to cry.

Sarah jumped off the couch to give me a hug. "Of course, we do." She touched my tummy. "This baby's father is Chris, your new love who loves you right back."

"Or it could be Elvis Presley's child," Mark said, rejoining the conversation.

"Mark!" I exclaimed. "Are you saying you believe me?" I felt a rush of hope.

"First of all, Maggie, Chris is a great guy and should be the father of this baby," Mark answered. "That's what's right and makes the most sense. But I was just thinking about wormholes."

"Wormholes," Sarah said, sarcastically.

"Wormholes, as in outer space?" I asked him.

"Wormholes are like tunnels that could, in theory, join two separate periods of time and allow passage from one to the other." I was loving this. "Scientists have proven that time travel to the future happens, such as astronauts in outer space, but time travel to the past is much more complicated because it throws off the laws of cause and effect. It's like you going back to a time before you were born. It creates a paradox."

Sarah and I tried to follow him. "It's complicated stuff, I know," he added. "But! Listen. Wormholes are very unstable." He leaned forward, his enthusiasm building. "Maggie, you said your portal was not in the hotel room where it was the first time you visited.

Wormholes keep changing. They can blink in and out of existence, which could explain why it was there and then it wasn't."

"Will it come back?" I asked, anxiously. "Could we find it again?"

"Maybe," he replied. "Like I said, it's complex. And nearly impossible."

"Well, nearly impossible could mean slightly possible, and if that's the case, I'm going with you, Maggie," Sarah chimed in. "I want to go shopping in the 1960s!"

"That's why I invited you two here!" I said, enthusiastically. "Mark, I knew you'd figure something out. Let's plan a trip to Memphis. The three of us. Let's go back to the hotel and look around some more. We just might find the portal, I mean, *wormhole*, and I can try to get back to Elvis!"

"Not so fast," Mark said. "Slow down." His expression was serious. "Did you hear me say that wormholes are unstable?"

"Yes, but …" I replied.

"No buts," Mark continued. "Maggie, you're pregnant. Chris is most likely the father. Are you thinking about what could happen? Let's say that we find the wormhole, which is an extreme long shot, but let's say we do and you're able to go back in time. Do you realize the ramifications if you don't come back?"

"I'll come back. I did last time."

"Listen to me!" Mark raised his voice.

"Uh oh, brother's getting pissed," Sarah interjected.

"If we find the wormhole, there's absolutely no guarantee it won't move again, or blink out of existence, and you'd be trapped in the past!" He focused on me. "Are you prepared to have a baby in the 1960s? First, your chances of a successful delivery would decrease. Second, there weren't as many single mothers back then—you'd practically be an outcast. Who would provide for you and the baby? And, what about never seeing Chris or your family again?" He paused. "It's a little selfish."

"I am not selfish!" I shouted back at him.

"It's a little selfish," Sarah agreed, taking a sip of her wine.

"Sarah!" I yelled.

"Take it easy." Mark took a breath before continuing. "I'm not trying to upset you, Maggie, I just want you to think—think hard—about your decision. I know you want to see Elvis. Heck, I'd like to meet the guy. *But you are pregnant*." He emphasized each word of his last sentence.

I was trying not to cry. I thought I had sold them on helping me. Sarah tried to smooth things out. "OK, Mark, you've said your piece. You've given Maggie a lot to think about. Me, too, if I go with her. And we'll think about this heavy stuff. Right, sis?"

"Yes, of course," I responded, then added, "With the exception of just learning about a wormhole, I've been thinking about this time travel thing for five months now."

The three of us were silent for a time, lost in our thoughts. Sarah, again, made a peace offering. "Mark, we'll go to Memphis and look around for the wormhole. If we find it, Maggie and I will give it a try and if it works, we'll come right back."

I looked at my brother to see what how he would respond. After a moment, he looked at Sarah and said, "Coming right back means no shopping spree."

"No shopping spree," Sarah replied. Behind her back, her fingers were crossed.

Mark finally conceded. "Alright." He looked at me. "What are we going to tell Chris about our sudden road trip?"

I looked at my brother, then my sister. "That's on me. I'll think of something."

CHAPTER 10

What Now, What Next, Where To

We decided on the second half of May, after comparing calendars and finding a weekend when we could go to Memphis together. I checked my Elvis encyclopedia and saw that he had leisure time at Graceland, which meant that, if we successfully traveled to 1961, the King would be in his castle. I was five months pregnant, and thanks to my tight young stomach, not showing very much.

Lucky for me, Chris had to work a weekend story. I told him I needed another Memphis fix, and my siblings wanted to go and have their big sis show them around. He didn't question that; he'd given up on any possibility that I actually time traveled. He was mostly concerned with me being careful. I told him I would enjoy everything sober, regardless of what Mark and Sarah would do.

I felt bad about not telling Chris the real reason we were going. I know that makes me a bad girlfriend, but if he knew I was about to attempt time travel, he would surely have prevented it.

Mark drove and Sarah sat up front because she often gets carsick. He had packed our favorite snacks for the road: Doritos and cheese popcorn for me; ranch-flavored Corn Nuts for Sarah and Jelly Belly Jelly Beans for him. I thought we all might get carsick after sharing.

Instead, I snoozed part of the way.

We had an interesting conversation, about how Mark would attempt to find the wormhole. He had been researching weather disturbances—pulses of energy moving through the atmosphere—and using Google Earth to pin their exact locations. He had a theory that he may be able to detect a similar atmospheric interference emanating from a wormhole, if one was still at the hotel. His laptop was loaded with research, weather radar and Google Earth. I was glad I convinced him to help me.

When we arrived at the Days Inn Graceland, I couldn't help but get some of those same old nostalgic feelings, with the sounds of Elvis Radio coming from the speakers and the guitar-shaped swimming pool. We checked in to Room 222, again, and I jokingly told the front desk attendant that superstition was the reason I kept requesting the same room.

Sarah and Mark, on the other hand, were not nostalgic. "This is … quaint," she said.

"It looks like a museum threw up," he added.

"Very funny," I replied. "It's perfectly themed for Elvis fans. Just … play along."

"OK," Sarah said.

Mark added with an eyeroll, "Whatever you say, sis."

We let ourselves into Room 222 and I headed straight for the other side of the far bed. Sarah grabbed my arm. "Not so fast, sister. I need to freshen up. Don't you disappear anywhere yet."

"I won't. But I'm dying to know if it's there again."

"We're gonna know soon enough," Mark said. He unzipped his bag and started setting up his laptop.

Sarah softened and looked me in the eyes. "Take a breath, sis. Let's transform ourselves into 1960s fashion mavens!" She rubbed my arm and smiled. "You never know who's waiting on the other side."

"OK. You go first." I motioned to the bathroom and she grabbed her things and went in.

I sat on the other bed and stared at the wall. "It doesn't look like a time portal, that's for sure," I said, then sighed. "But I don't remember it looking peculiar the last time, or the time before."

"Mmmhmm," Mark mumbled in response, as he logged into his laptop.

"Do you think this will work?" I ask him.

"We're going to give it a try." He inserted something into the side of his laptop.

"Thanks, brother." I waited impatiently for my sister to get ready.

Sarah returned from the bathroom looking, indeed, transformed. She had teased her shoulder-length, straight brown hair and curled up the ends, and put on a legitimate dress: the top half was short-sleeve with royal blue and white vertical stripes. At the waist was a horizontal belt-like attachment with belt loops and two big white buttons. The lower half was solid blue. She was wearing royal blue pumps and spun around like a runway model.

"Perfect!" I told her. "You look like you're auditioning for that new show *Mad Men.*"

"Why, thank you! Now it's your turn."

I tried to follow her lead; however, I always felt frumpier. I couldn't do as much with my hair—my curls would not cooperate. I did manage to tie them cutely into submission using a green scarf as a headband. It matched the outfit Sarah had chosen for me, keeping in mind my growing tummy. It looked like a top under a jumper but was actually a dress. The jumper portion was emerald green. The mock-neck top with three-quarter length sleeves had bold horizontal stripes in emerald, red, navy and white. A long zipper ran down the back. My pumps were navy blue.

I stepped out of the bathroom, worried what my sister would think. "It's not *Mad Men*, but it may pass for *Partridge Family.*"

"You look great! I love it!" Sarah said.

I turned my back to her. "Then finish my zipper and let's do this."

"I think we're ready to give it a go," Mark said, oblivious to our new wardrobe.

"Just a second," Sarah halted. "Tell me again what it's going to feel like. Am I going to fall, or get dizzy?"

"Sarah ..." I interrupted.

She did the same. "I'm not making fun of it, Maggie. Or you. I just want to know what to expect."

"Alright." I paused. "It's going to feel a little like falling, like being wobbly on your legs."

She closed her eyes, submitting to the moment. "Falling. Wobbly," she repeated. "OK. Do we go together? Or one after the other?"

"I'll go first. And if I disappear, count to three and follow me."

Suddenly, she reached out and hugged me. "I love you, sis."

I returned her embrace. "I love you, too."

Mark rolled his eyes at us. "Please stop and go back to Graceland."

"We love you, too, Mark," we both said in unison.

A step at a time, I made my way toward the space between the bed and the wall. My heart quickened its pace. Was I about to go back to Graceland? I took another step. Would I get to see Elvis again? I was almost there. I turned around and saw that Sarah had inched her way toward me, a few steps behind. Mark was manning his station. I took the final step.

And nothing happened. *Again!* The surprise caused me to take a step backward and I bumped into my sister. "What the —!" I exclaimed, then jumped forward to the space where the portal used to be. "Noooo!" I jumped up and down a few times.

Sarah reached for me. "Maggie, calm down." She looked me in the eye. "The baby? You have to stay calm."

"I don't want to stay calm—I want to scream!" I went on a rant. "I want to see Elvis, I want to tell him I'm pregnant and I want everyone to believe me that this wasn't some, some … story I made up!"

"I'm sorry, Maggie. Come here, sit down on the bed and catch your breath. This anger can't be good for you." Sarah motioned me to the bed nearby. I obliged her but I was still fuming.

"I don't understand!" I said. "It was here, it really was. And then it was gone. Now it's still gone." I was losing steam. Sarah put her arm around me.

"Mark," I pleaded, looking at my brother, who was quietly obsessing over his laptop. "You said if it's a wormhole, they're unstable and they move around."

"Yes, I did say that."

"Well, what if it didn't move very far? What if it's around here somewhere, in this room, in another room, or somewhere else around this hotel. Can we try to find it? I mean, we're here, we're ready. Can we?"

"Maggie, if there's a wormhole around here somewhere, in an obvious place, people would fall into it and disappear."

"It could be in a place where people don't walk that often, like when I found it in this narrow space between the bed and the wall." I began begging. "Please, Mark? You've got your theory and your research. Can't we at least get up and walk the property a bit?"

As if he didn't hear me, Mark continued his train of thought. "And if the wormhole moved in the present time, that could mean it moved in the past, too." A pause. "It might not be in the Graceland basement anymore." Another pause. "It might not be at Graceland at all."

"Fine!" I was getting angry again. "If you're not going to help me, I'll go by myself." I got up and headed for the door.

"C'mon, Mark, let's help our sister," Sarah said, getting up to follow me. "We agreed to help her."

After a moment, Mark said, "Alright. Let's try." He followed us out of the room, laptop open and running.

We must have looked a little strange, three people in a row, searching for something. I took the lead, followed by Sarah and Mark with his laptop. I laughed and turned to them, "I bet people think we're trying to find the hotel wifi."

"Not necessary," Mark said. "I've got an air card."

"*Air card*, fancy!" Sarah teased.

We walked all of the hallways, past all of the rooms, on all floors, front and back. While we were on the middle floor in the back of the hotel, we neared a couple of rooms that had a maid's cart in front. The doors to both rooms were open. I turned to my siblings. "Here's a couple of rooms we might be able to sneak into."

"Maggie," Sarah began. "Don't get in trouble."

"I won't. If I get caught, I'll just act like I mistakenly went to the wrong room." I peeked inside the room closest to us and it appeared to be empty. "You guys stay outside. I'm going to go have a look around."

And I did. For some reason, the maid seemed to be cleaning the bathroom with the door closed. I heard talking. Maybe she was on the phone? I tiptoed around the room and made my way to the space between the bed and the wall. I gave a thought as to what would happen if I found the wormhole and suddenly disappeared. The maid wouldn't find me, but would Mark and Sarah come looking?

My stealthy search of this room was unfruitful, though, and I went back outside. I shrugged at my siblings and headed to the other open room next door. "I don't think there's a maid in that one," Sarah whispered.

There wasn't. So I did another room search. It was also unsuccessful. Damn! When I came back outside, Sarah was there but Mark was not. "Where's Mark?" I asked.

"Down at the end of the hallway," Sarah replied.

I made a beeline for my brother. He was sitting cross-legged on the ground, staring intensely at his computer on his lap. Maybe he found something! I got excited and rushed to him. "Mark! What did you find?"

I must have interrupted his concentration because he jumped when he heard my voice. And he did something strange: he closed his laptop.

"Mark! What are you doing?"

"Nothing. It was nothing." He was acting weird. "I'm sorry, Maggie. I tried. We tried. We can't search every inch of this hotel, but even if we could, it doesn't look like we're going to find your portal."

Sarah had caught up to us and heard what he said. She came to my side. "I'm sorry, too, sis. I know how much this means to you."

I was quiet, wondering why Mark was in such a hurry when I walked up to him. “Mark, you'd better not be hiding something from me.”

“I'm not,” he replied. “Chill out.”

Sarah interrupted us. “What do you say we go back to the room and get ready for a night out on the town?”

“The room,” I replied.

“Yes, Maggie, our room. Let's go back and relax for a bit. Then we'll go out tonight and have some fun on Beale Street.”

“We forgot to search the rest of our room!” I realized and made a hasty return.

Like before with Chris, I searched every inch of Room 222. Mark and Sarah came back and watched me but didn't assist. “If I go through somewhere in this room, you two had better wait for me to come back.” My threat didn't matter, though, because another thorough search did not reveal a wormhole.

I was disappointed again, and crawled under the covers in an attempt to disappear. Sarah joined me on the bed and offered words of comfort. Mark tried to cheer me up by finding something funny to watch on TV. I closed my eyes and tried to ignore them. Eventually, they convinced me we needed to go out and have some fun. I wasn't in the mood, nor could I drink alcohol, but I loved Beale Street.

Sarah was hilarious; she had a bit much to drink. “Hello, Memphis!” she shouted repeatedly as we prowled Beale; she got some “hellos” back. At B.B. King's, she took off for the dance floor. The music by the house band was fabulous. Though I felt defeated after our failed attempt at time travel, I couldn't help but get into the beat.

“Who needs a freaking wormhole when you can have this!” Mark shouted at me while we kept an eye on Sarah. I made a face at him. He was a little tipsy, too. It had already been decided that pregnant big sister was the designated driver. “What were you thinking?

Trying to go back to the past while you're pregnant with Chris' child."

"Why don't you go dance with Sarah," I yelled back. "And besides, we don't for sure know who the father is."

"Maybe *you* don't, but I do. You and *Chris* are having a baby."

"Is that so? I'm glad my little brother has it all figured out."

"I do! The King of Rock & Roll didn't get you pregnant. That was just a good dream."

"Shut up, Mark." I responded. "I'm done with this for tonight."

I should be done with this for good. Raise this baby with Chris as the father. Science could prove his paternity if needed.

Mark had taken my advice and was out on the dance floor with Sarah. Watching them made me laugh and I wondered why I ever involved them in a crusade that only I could understand.

Well after midnight, back in Room 222, Mark was wide awake, waiting for his sisters to fall asleep. He needed an opportunity to get back to his theory, by himself, because he thought he detected something earlier today at the end of the hallway.

Sarah passed out quickly. It took Maggie a while to get comfortable, then she finally dozed off. It would be an incredible discovery, a wormhole to another place in time, but Mark had no interest in sending his pregnant sister there. This would be his secret.

Quietly, he got out of bed and grabbed his laptop. Making sure he had a room key in his pocket, he snuck out. At the end of the hallway, he booted up the laptop and opened weather radar and Google Earth through his air card. "Let's see if I can recreate what happened this afternoon," he whispered to himself. He'd found a small atmospheric disturbance in the immediate area of the hotel. With Maggie desperately prowling for the portal, he'd decided to not to move around with his computer and attract her attention. When she'd coming running, he'd shut it down.

Now, Mark discovered some type of disturbance nearby. "Let's take a little walk and see what happens to this pulse of energy." On the way back toward the room, it faded out. He went up to the third floor and took the same walk. He got a low ping at the north end of the hallway. He went down and walked the first-floor hallway. At the north end, below floors two and three, the ping increased. "Aha!" he said, a little too loud, but no one was around at this hour.

His laptop leading the way, Mark kept walking the property. The ping was the strongest when he rounded the corner out back. "Whoa!" It was the side wall of the building, bare of any hotel rooms or windows, an empty, grassy lot next to it. "What have we here?" He paused to gather his thoughts. If he was about to fall into a wormhole, he wondered if he should take his computer with him. He doubted it would work, if he could even hold on to it in a wormhole. Probably better than leaving it behind, to be found by the hotel or his sisters when they came looking for him.

Decision made. He'd bring the laptop with him. Holding it a bit tighter, he made his way along the side wall. About halfway there, his right leg about fell out from under him. "What the…?" He toppled sideways. Sure that he was about to hit the ground, he braced for impact, strong-arming his computer.

He felt like he was in an elevator full of too much air, like he and the air were jockeying for the limited space. His ears popped, he was dizzy. Was the elevator racing downward? The ground underneath him was hard. He thought he smelled wood. He realized his eyes were squeezed shut. Willing himself to open them, he noticed the scene was not the same. He was in a squatting position, low to the ground. He looked down at the laptop he'd been white knuckling. The screen was black. He closed it.

Mark was in a narrow space. To his right, there was a wall. To his left, a wood pile. "Holy shit!" He figured he needed to move or he would fall back into the wormhole. But which way? He chose to move left, closer to the logs. Nothing happened. Still squatting, he looked across the wood pile. He placed his laptop on the ground next to him.

Wherever he was, they needed wood for something. With a pounding heart, Mark willed his scientific mind to take over. "I can breathe this air. I'm on solid ground. The climate is moderate. It's dark. Is it nighttime?" He looked around some more as his eyes adjusted to the dark. It wasn't the same hotel side lot that he started in. It looked like a big yard. He was near the back of a house. Beyond him, he could see a swimming pool, a fountain area, a barn, a couple of small buildings, and a carport full of cars. "Wherever I am, they've got some dough."

Mark stood up. His knees were a bit wobbly. He made his way over to the cars and one in particular caught his eye. He walked closer to get a better look in the darkness. "Nice Cadillac. Is it … pink?" Suddenly, his mind cleared, as though he'd been slapped in the head. He realized he was quite possibly standing in the backyard of Elvis Presley's Graceland! He heard laughing coming from inside the house. He ducked down. If Elvis comes walking out here right now, I'm in trouble, he thought. He'll call the police, they'll arrest me and take me away.

Acting on instinct, Mark scrambled back to where his laptop lay on the ground. He scooped it up and the sounds of the group inside grew louder. Were they headed this way? He'd better act fast. Make a run for who knows where or go back where he came from. Who knew if he'd successfully get off the property before he was spotted, or if Elvis would be a nice guy about finding a stranger on his property.

Mark could hear his pulse in his ears. Instinct took over. Crouching down as far as possible, and hugging his computer, he tiptoed hurriedly toward the wood pile, back to the familiar. He scrambled behind it, staying as close to the logs as possible because he wasn't exactly sure where the entrance to the wormhole was. He stayed low and tried to catch his breath.

The back door opened and a group of young people tumbled out—guys and girls, talking, joking, and laughing. Mark ducked down completely, grateful for the darkness and the cover the stack of logs provided. A girl said, “I’m hungry for some buttered popcorn.” A guy said, “Honey, I’ll share a bucket with you any day.” The next voice that Mark heard made him edge his way up to take a peek.

“Pat, ride in the back seat of my car with your fiancé, will you?” he said. “You two ain’t married yet so I’ve got to keep my eye on Red to make sure he behaves.” The response was laughter.

It was him. Elvis Presley! He had his arm around a petite girl with long dark hair and they were making their way to the carport. Maggie was right! She discovered a passage through time. A damn good one at that—a passage to the King of Rock ‘n Roll.

The sounds of several car engines filled the night. One by one, they pulled out of the carport and drove around the house, headed away for what sounded like a movie night.

Crouched behind the wood pile, Mark’s head was spinning. His inner science geek wanted to stay and explore this new world. But what if the wormhole shifted again and he couldn’t go back? Did he want to get stuck here? No. He needed to go back to the present, to study wormholes and time travel. He would keep this from his sisters, especially the one who thinks she’s carrying Elvis’ baby. He would return some day, to document and prove.

Mark laid down on his back and stared at the dark sky. *Elvis Presley, wow!* Slowly, he edged away from the wood pile, toward the wall, hugging his laptop to his chest. Mark’s final thought before his ears started popping and his body fell into the dizzying space of the wormhole: *Could I be as famous as him some day?*

CHAPTER 11

My Happiness

Life is complicated, but beautiful nonetheless. There's something about being pregnant that prompts you to get your ducks in a row.

I had to face a difficult truth after two failed attempts to go back to Graceland: I was not going to see Elvis again. I believed with my entire soul that my time with him was real; however, I was unable to recreate it so it was time to move on. I had a man who was *here* and loved me. Chris accepted me for who I am and the experiences I've had. Elvis would live forever in my heart.

As my doctor predicted, my pregnancy was normal. I didn't have anything to compare it to; Mom was gone and couldn't give motherly advice. I got a little scared about getting sick in the morning but friends and co-workers assured me it would pass. It was *the worst*. Some days I didn't feel like myself until the afternoon. I survived on sparkling water and crackers.

When I reached my second trimester, the morning sickness subsided. It was like a new lease on life. It seemed healthy to be pregnant, even though I was getting fatter by the day. I was overwhelmed, in a good way, by the progress of a little person growing inside of me. Who would he or she grow up to be?

I decided not to learn the baby's gender. Chris was fine with that. We'd made a lot of progress since the night I told him I was pregnant. He'd come to terms with the baby's last name being Coyle, at least for now. Even though I was Catholic, and my "super-Catholic" relatives didn't agree, I couldn't handle a wedding while I was pregnant—it was just too much. Chris and I were committed to the life we were building and would deal with marriage later.

With about five weeks to go, I hit another milestone—my 30th birthday—on the 30th anniversary of Elvis' death. August 16, 1977: the King of Rock 'n Roll died and I was born.

Chris made my 30th extra special. I was joining him in the new decade; he had turned 30 in December 2006, the same month we went to Graceland and I went back in time. I had told him I didn't want a party, so he cleverly went behind the scenes at my job to fill my office with black balloons. It was funny—my employee and I had to pop a bunch of them with pencils so I could get to my desk!

Chris also left a beautiful birthday card on the kitchen counter, promising "more to come." When I got home from work that night, there were 30 red roses in a vase, along with a selection of my favorite "pregnant" foods: asiago bagels, beef jerky, oatmeal crème pies and carrot cake. He took me to my favorite Italian restaurant for dinner and read me a list of 30 reasons why he loves me. One of the top 10 was how I chose to love him over Elvis. Like I said, we'd made progress.

September 22, 2007

Before I knew it, it was time. Nine months since I made love to Elvis Presley, followed by Chris Streater. I was about to join the line of women with paternity dilemmas but was in a league of my own when it came to time-traveling mamas with baby daddy issues.

Me going into labor will go down in history at my job because it started there. My water broke on the walk from my office to the bathroom. It was the first time our maintenance team was ever called to clean up *that* kind of spill. *Mortifying!*

My labor pains came on pretty quickly after that. I called Chris and he left work immediately. My boss and a few others waited with me in the lobby. One of them was extra attentive to time my contractions. I was nervous and pained. They told me I had plenty of time to get to the hospital.

I barely made it. They were waiting for me at the entrance with a wheelchair and things moved rapidly after that. When they saw I was in active labor, they took me straight to a delivery room. I was scared. Chris held my hand and tried to calm me.

It doesn't matter how you prepare for the pain—it hurts! My mom used to say it's like "shitting a watermelon" and she wasn't lying. Luckily, I wasn't in labor for long. I've heard stories about hours and hours of walking the halls and waiting and pushing. I pushed three or four times, and then she arrived. "It's a girl!" they announced. Seven pounds, 10 ounces and 21 inches of healthy, beautiful baby girl.

When they placed my newborn daughter in my arms, I was in Heaven. I was holding a precious angel and sure of three things: I love Chris. I'll always love Elvis, and I'm head over heels in love with this new person. "Amazing," was all I managed to say.

Alongside me, Chris quietly asked, "Now that you've seen her, what's her name?"

"Grace," I replied, without a doubt. "Amazing Grace."

He laughed. "Would Grace be her middle name?"

"No." I knew her full name by heart. "Grace Christina Coyle." A pause. "Christina after you. And maybe someday Streater." We kissed.

"Alright then." Taking her tiny hand with his index finger, he added, "Hello, Grace Christina. Welcome to the world."

As if in response, she tightened her grip on his finger and looked up at me. Grace Christina Coyle stole my heart and became my number one priority.

Two days later, it was time to go home. I was ready. I was done with the bright lights, smells and constant noise of the hospital. Grace was doing well. They rolled us out in a wheelchair to wait for Chris to pick us up.

Holding my tiny baby, staring at her beautiful face while she slept, smelling her baby smell, I thought, "Everything is as it should be." Followed immediately by "or not?" I was haunted by the possibility that Grace belonged to Elvis, too.

Chris pulled up in his chariot and, thankfully, interrupted my thoughts. He jumped out and came over to greet me. "Hey sweetie! How are you? And how's our baby girl?"

"We're both doing great and ready to go home!" I replied.

We strapped Grace safely into her car seat. We held hands on the way home and didn't say much. I think we were both in shock as reality sank in.

When we got home, we moved everything in. I was still sore and moving slowly. Chris was very sweet. We put Grace in the center of our bed and laid down on each side of her, staring at this tiny miracle. "What do we do now?" Chris looked at me and asked.

Good question.

PART TWO

Four Years Later

CHAPTER 12

Funny How Time Slips Away

September 22, 2011

"Make a wish, Gracie!" someone said from around the dining room table.

Followed by someone else, "Don't tell anybody or it won't come true."

The adorable curly-headed blonde, dressed in a shiny white party dress with black polka dots, black sash with red flower accent and matching red hair bow, scrunched her eyes closed, no doubt dreaming up a birthday wish. Then, she opened her baby blues and blew out four candles with one big breath. Applause followed.

"I can't believe my baby is 4 years old!" I said to the small group of family and friends we'd assembled to celebrate Grace's birthday. The theme was 'black and white,' inspired by Elvis' black and white movies. Yes, I'm raising a little Elvis fan.

"I'm not a baby anymore, Mama," Grace chided. "I'm 4, and that's old enough to go to Graceland. You said."

"Yes, I did." Little did she know I had a surprise planned for her soon—a birthday trip to Graceland.

"That's right, honey, you're a little lady now," Chris said, standing next to me, rubbing my back. "Where did the time go?" he asked me quietly.

I leaned into him. "Indeed."

Where *did* the time go? They weren't kidding when they said that having a baby changes your life forever. Grace is the best thing that ever happened to me, a beautiful gift from above. Together, Chris and I have adored her development and milestones. From that first nerve-wracking bath to her first smile and first laugh. Hilarious, messy endeavors with first solid foods. Rolling over, sitting up, crawling, standing, walking—all so special to watch Grace learn to do. Her first word was "baba" for bottle. "Mama" and "Poppy" came later. She calls Chris "Poppy." Grandpa Coyle, my dad, is "Paw Paw."

Of course, it wasn't all sunshine and rainbows. The heavenly smell of a clean baby is one thing, but poop and puke are another—sickening. I had to toughen up through diaper blowouts and upset tummies. Sleep deprivation was worse—the most tired I've been in my life. We jumped for joy when she started sleeping through the night. We gritted *our* teeth when she cut hers. We learned a lot about patience, especially during Grace's terrible twos.

We're still not married—yet. I hate to go into it; I know I've disappointed the Catholic family and it bothers me, too. But there was a snag in our relationship. Chris' ex wife resurfaced through social media and reconnected with him. Behind my back, he met her for dinner one night, thinking it was just two old friends reuniting. She had other intentions, though, and it got a little messy. Chris told me about it; I got upset about it. When I accused him of cheating, he brought up my never-ending love for Elvis. That put a wedge between us for a while. We focused on Grace and eventually worked it out. The ex moved on when she saw that Chris wasn't going to leave Grace and me.

How could anyone leave Grace? She is one cool kid. Beautiful, smart, funny, loving, creative. I wouldn't trade Grace and these experiences with her for anything else. I love her most of all. I'm so proud to be her mother. I'm blessed to love her and raise her, and witness the woman she'll grow up to be. She brought Chris and I closer together. Our love deepened because we went through good times and bad times together.

If I'm being *completely* honest, not many days go by without remembering *another* best thing that ever happened to me—Elvis—

and wondering if Grace also belongs to him. This question lurks at the edges of my thoughts. It's not fair to Chris—he loves Grace as if she was his own, and she certainly could be. Once in a while, though, a look flashes across Grace's face, or she says something a certain way, and I'm reminded of Elvis.

Like the other day. Grace was making tea party invitations at her little table in her room. I had passed by to check on her and she was happy, singing and talking to herself. Not much later, I heard several thuds and hurried back to her room. Two of the chairs had been knocked over. There were crayons and paper everywhere. She was standing in the middle of it all with wads of paper in each hand. "Grace, honey! What's the matter? What happened?" I'd asked her.

"I hate these invitations! They're ugly and stupid!"

"It's OK. We can start over. I'll help you make some new ones."

"No. I don't need your help," she'd fumed. "I think it's time for you to leave."

That look in her eyes, and the fire within them, gave me chills. I'd seen that look before. I'd felt its anger.

It was times like these that made me wonder who her father truly was.

CHAPTER 13

Speedway

October 1965

Elvis and his entourage were back at Graceland. The "Elvis-mobile" Greyhound bus and a variety of Cadillacs were parked out back. The caravan had returned after a busy year of shooting *Harum Scarum*, *Frankie and Johnny* and *Paradise, Hawaiian Style* in California and Hawaii. Three movies in seven months.

Elvis played as hard as he worked. The spring and summer of '65 were spent aboard motorcycles. As with everything, Elvis went BIG. He didn't just buy himself a bike, he bought Bonneville Triumphs for each member of his Memphis Mafia. They roared around LA in a biker brigade Elvis dubbed "El's Angels." It wasn't all playtime for Jerry Schilling, though. He was thrown off of his Bonneville in a traffic accident and spent a couple of weeks in the hospital. Jerry was dealing with considerable pain as he recovered.

There were new toys at Graceland, too. Elvis was into go karts. Loud, low riders with lots of power. For a few days now, they revved up noise and fumes all over the property as the guys chased Elvis up and down the driveway in their perennially competitive atmosphere.

The days were getting shorter, but dusk didn't stop Elvis. He was in a good mood, had a full belly and wanted to race. "To the go karts," he ordered, coming down the stairs in an all-black outfit—black pants and boots, black leather jacket over black mock turtleneck, even black racing gloves.

The guys jumped to attention, as usual, and readied for another adventure. They headed out back where a line of eight go karts were parked in a row, keys in the ignitions, ready to be fired up.

"You comin', Jerry?" Elvis turn back and asked him as he headed out the back door.

"Um, no, boss," he said, regretfully. "I'm hurtin' kinda bad today so I think I'd better just watch." Admitting that to Elvis made him feel as bad as his body did. "I can wave the starting flag?" he offered.

"Sure. And we'll do some more 'healing power' later. We gotta get you back to 100 percent." Through voracious reading about philosophy, Elvis had come to believe in the healing power of the hands and tried, somewhat successfully, to pull Jerry's pain away from his injured back.

The guys cranked up their go karts. "Wait up!" Elvis yelled and jumped into his and turned on the engine. It was loud, really loud, as they all paraded around front and lined up for a race. Jerry stood on the front porch with a few flags in his hands. He raised the green one and the engines purred in unison. When he dropped it, they accelerated and took off down the driveway, one after the other. Elvis, of course, in the lead.

Priscilla was watching from inside the front door. Grandma Presley walked up behind her. "When are they going to stop that infernal racket?"

"Oh, Grandma! You scared me. With all of the noise, I didn't hear you walk up."

"It's no wonder. I need earplugs around here lately."

"Well, stay inside because it's much louder out there. And smelly. I can hardly stand those fumes!"

"Boys," the old woman replied.

"Yes indeed," Priscilla agreed. "They're boys more often than they're men."

There were several rounds of green flags followed by checkered flags. Elvis won most of the time; the guys were smart that way. Sonny West pulled off a victory but knew better than to try it again. On a non-racing lap down the driveway, Sonny slowed to get a look at the pretty girls. The noise had drawn Elvis' fans outside closer to the gate.

When Elvis slowed his go kart at the gate, they grew more enthusiastic. He was always nice to his fans—polite, shaking hands and signing autographs—but not every time. Today, he stayed in his go kart.

Sonny pulled up beside him. Over the hum of their idling engines, he asked, "What do you say, boss, how about we let in that gorgeous red head and her two friends?" He nodded in their direction. They were grinning and elbowing each other on the other side of the gate.

Elvis made eye contact with the three girls, which sent them squealing. "Sure, Sonny," he replied. "But get 'em up to the porch safely, without any of 'em gettin' run over." With that, he revved up his engine, waved to his fans and took off up the driveway.

The guys ran a couple of more races. Sonny had climbed off the go kart he was driving to flirt with the girls on the front porch. Joe Esposito had entered the race. He didn't win, though; Elvis was the lone victor. He called a halt to their antics just as it got dark. The group made their way around back, some in go karts, some on foot.

Priscilla and the other ladies were waiting outside the house. Sonny introduced Elvis to his new friends. "Elvis, this is Julie and Donna."

"Nice to meet you," Elvis said, shaking each of their hands. The girls tried to play it cool but their amazement was audible.

Putting an arm around the red head's shoulder, Sonny continued. "And this is Maggie." It was obvious she was Sonny's favorite. "Girls, this is my boss, Elvis Presley."

Suddenly, Elvis got feisty. He didn't shake her hand like he did the others. "Maggie, huh?" he said, sounding aggravated by this simple introduction.

"Yes. Nice to meet you, Elvis," she replied, shyly.

"I'm sorry, but I don't like the name Maggie." Red overheard this and walked closer to the conversation. He wasn't fond of a certain

Maggie, although this was a different girl. "How 'bout we give you a nickname," Elvis continued. "Like … Red." Noticing Red, he realized that would be repetitive. "Or … Little Red. Little Red Riding Hood!" He made himself laugh. The group standing around was not sure what was going on, but they laughed, too.

Maggie's cheeks now matched her hair. Clearly embarrassed, she replied, "Sure, Elvis, that would be fine."

Seeming to snap out of it, Elvis invited group to the house. "Let's go inside and get something to eat. I worked up another appetite."

The guys and girls headed inside. Priscilla caught up to Elvis on the lawn. "What was that Maggie thing about, Elvis?" she asked. "Is she someone from before?" Priscilla liked to believe that all other women in Elvis' life came before her.

"I don't want to talk about it, and I don't want to hear that name!" he said, his agitation returning. "Do I make myself clear, woman?"

"I'm sorry, Elvis," Priscilla said, feeling scolded. "You don't have to get all moody."

He stopped in his tracks and glared at her with fire in his eyes. "Moody? You're calling me Moody?! Well, I don't like that name either, so don't call me that again!"

"I'm sorry, Elvis," she said again, as he stormed through the back door. Under her breath, she muttered, "Moody's not a name, it's an emotion."

CHAPTER 14

Steppin' Out of Line

Uncle Mark was cutting the *Jailhouse Rock* birthday cake, complete with a little Elvis figurine. Grace was directing him. "I want the piece with Elvis on top."

"Of course, birthday girl. You get exactly the slice you want," he replied.

"Maybe we can cut some tiny pieces of cake for my next tea party! Can we, Mama?" she asked, looking at me.

"Let's first make sure that everyone here gets a piece of cake, then we'll see how much is left for you and your animals."

"Animals!" she balked. "Mama, my tea party guests are not animals!" She laughed. "That would be so messy, an animal tea party." More giggling.

"Let's make sure everyone gets Jelly Bellys, too," Mark said to Grace. He was proud of his theme party jelly beans—in black, white and red colors—and teased us about some wild flavors like black pepper, spoiled milk and earthworm.

"Alright, but you better give me cherry and vanilla Jelly Bellys—those other ones are gross," Grace declared.

While Mark handled distribution of dessert, I noticed Sarah trying to get my attention, discreetly. I went over to her and she pulled me into the hallway.

"We need to talk," she whispered.

That didn't sound good. "What's up?"

She paused. "I found out something, about Mark." She nodded back toward the dining room.

"What's going on?" I looked toward Mark's direction, too. "Is he

OK?"

"Yeah, he's fine." A pause. "Maybe we should just talk later, somewhere more private, away from Mark. And Chris."

"What does this have to do with Chris? Spill it, sis. What has Mark gotten himself into now?"

She just looked at me.

"Sarah!"

"Calm down. Just listen, OK?"

"Yes. OK."

She pulled me farther down the hallway and took a deep breath. "Mark invited me to happy hour last night, with his friends. You know me, I'm always up for a few drinks with fun people—guys—so I went. It was a good time! Mark got kind of drunk."

"So far, nothing new or earth shattering."

"True, except …" she trailed off.

"Except what?" I was getting exasperated.

"Except he got a little mouthy about his science stuff and said something kind of shocking. His friends just laughed at him and didn't take him seriously. But he locked eyes with me and told me to keep my mouth shut."

"What did he say?"

She just stared at me again. Then said, "He went back in time. To Graceland."

"What?!"

"Yep. A long time ago. Do you remember when we went to Memphis, before Grace was born, and he tried to help us go back?"

"Of course, I remember! What do you mean, he went back?"

"He found the portal. After he told us to give up, *he* found it, and went back."

"Are you serious?"

"Yes. He didn't stay long, didn't find out what year it was, but he did get back to Graceland."

"Oh my God. I'm going to kill him—with my bare hands."

"No, you're not. Because he swore me to secrecy."

"Right there in the bar, while he was drunk? That doesn't count."

"No, when I took him home. He rambled on about it in the car." She shifted in her seat. "Maggie, I've been debating whether to tell you. You can't do anything with this information."

I started to get emotional. "Did he … did he see Elvis?"

"Yes. He did. But Elvis didn't see him because he decided not to stay and not to tell us, because …"

"Because why?" I was near tears.

"Because you belong here with Chris and Grace, not in the past with Elvis."

"It's not his right to decide!" I slammed my hand on the wall. Now I was angry.

"He's your brother, and just wants what's best for you."

"How does *he* know what's best?" I hissed.

"Well, he's right, isn't he? You have a great life, here with all of us, not trapped somewhere in the past."

"Yes, I do. And I would never leave Grace, no matter what. Even if Elvis were her father."

"Mark mouthed off about proving paternity, too."

"He what?"

"He was going on about how famous he'd be if he could prove existence of a wormhole, or if Elvis was Grace's father. He's been studying time travel on and off ever since." She laughed. "Thank goodness those two girlfriends take up so much of his time."

I was dumbfounded. "How would Mark prove Elvis is Grace's father?"

"Don't ask me." She laughed again. "I'm telling you, he was drunk as a skunk, and it was all crazy talk."

I was still angry. "How dare he! He had no right to keep this from me. And he has no right meddling in my life."

"He's your brother, Maggie. He thinks it was the right move, not telling you. And maybe it was! You focused on your pregnancy and your relationship with Chris. You forgot about Elvis. You had an amazing baby girl."

"I never forgot about Elvis!" I interrupted her. "Never!"

She shook her head at me. "Maggie," was all she said.

"Sarah," I responded, sarcastically.

After a moment, she spoke again. "And besides …"

"Besides what?"

"It's been a long time. Things have changed. Mark said he tried to go back a second time and the wormhole wasn't there."

"*Wasn't* where?"

"Behind the hotel, near a wall on the side of the building. He found a pulse of energy and Google Earth directed him there." As soon as she said it, she covered her mouth.

"It moved! Mark said wormholes can move!" *Aha!* "Where did he find the portal in the past?"

Sarah leaned against the wall. "I shouldn't have told you. This was a bad idea."

"Where was the wormhole in the past?" I pleaded.

"Outside, behind the house. Mark didn't end up in the basement at Graceland, like you said you did."

"Wow," I said. "The wormhole moved in the past, *and* in the present."

"Right." Attempting to recover, she added, "So who knows where the wormhole could be by now, if it's even there at all."

"Who knows." I shrugged, in an attempt disguise what I was really thinking: *time for a road trip.*

CHAPTER 15

Runaway

October 2011

I was more determined than ever. I'm glad Sarah spilled the beans about what Mark did, because it was just the information, and kick in the ass, that I needed to try again.

This morning, Grace and I hit the road for Memphis. She was ecstatic. I had promised her a trip after she turned 4. I laughed to myself when I realized her first look at Graceland would possibly be as it existed in the early years of Elvis living there.

It wasn't easy, leaving town without Chris, not to mention my siblings. With Sarah, I played it off like it didn't matter. Sure, I got pissed off when she told me about Mark finding the portal and traveling back to Graceland, but my strategic brain took over and I tucked away my anger. I acted like I didn't care anymore—about Elvis or time travel. She didn't question my reactions.

I wondered, but didn't ask, if Sarah ever told Mark that I knew what he did. For the time being, I decided not to initiate any contact with Mark. It worked because he was never as good at staying in touch as I was.

Chris was a different matter. Grace and I lived with him. He was her Poppy; he was our family. This is where strategy came into play. I was of course itching to hit the road right away, but knew I had to go to Graceland without him. I scoured our calendars and found a time, in mid-October, when he would be out of town for a conference. Bingo.

"I've decided I'm going to take Grace to Memphis and Graceland, when you go to the newspaper conference," I'd announced one evening.

"Do you have to go then?" He'd responded. "I'd like to go, when she gets to see it for the first time."

"I was just thinking that I'd spare you having to do the complete tour again. You know she's going to want to see every bit of it."

"Yeah, but Grace at Graceland—that could be worth seeing."

It was then that Grace had come into the room and overheard our conversation. "Grace at Graceland! Mama, really? Are we going? When?" she'd enthused, jumping up and down.

Her excitement sealed the deal. Chris was a sucker for seeing her happy. He didn't put up a fight. It was settled. When he left town, so would we.

And here we were, about 20 miles until Elvis Presley Boulevard and the Days Inn Graceland. Grace was staring intensely at the pages of my Graceland guidebook. I looked at her through the rearview mirror. "You know, Grace, you're going to see those rooms in person, real soon."

"I know, Mama," she said. "I'm taking pictures of them with my brain, so I know my way around when we get there."

When we get there. I liked the sound of that.

We drove to the hotel, checked in and went to our room. I didn't request Room 222 like I had before. They gave us Room 223, which made me smile because that was the room Chris stayed in when we came here for his newspaper story.

Grace did what all kids do in hotel rooms—jumped on the bed. I chose the outfits we would change in to and put a couple more into a big tote bag. I packed a few other items: pajamas, makeup, a gift for Patsy and an envelope I may need if we reached our destination.

I changed into my ensemble for the day: red stretch pants with a long-sleeve navy blue top and black ankle boots. The top had red piping at the neckline, chest pocket, sleeves and waistline. "Grace, it's time to get changed." I had selected a red corduroy sleeveless jumper with pleats, over a white long-sleeve blouse with Peter Pan collar, plus white tights and black Mary Janes. "Then I want to talk to you about a few things before we leave for Graceland."

"I know, Mama," she said. "I have to be a good girl and follow the rules."

"Get changed." When we were both ready, I sat in the chair and pulled her on to my lap, facing me.

"Is it time to get on one of the Graceland buses, Mama?" she asked.

"No, Grace, we're going a different way," I replied.

"We're going to drive our car up the big driveway?"

"No. We're going to try something else." *Here're the part where I become a terrible mother.* "We're going to go outside the hotel, out back, and look for a wormhole. If we find it, we're going to walk into the wormhole to get to Graceland."

"A wormhole?" she asked, scrunching up her face inquisitively. "Worms are really little, Mama. We won't fit in a wormhole."

"This wormhole is special." My mind reached for an example she would understand. "Do you remember how Alice in Wonderland was able to travel through the rabbit hole and visit Wonderland, no matter what size she was?"

"Yes."

"Well, this will be a little like that. We need to have a little faith, make a wish, and then we'll be on our way to Graceland."

"Why can't we just take a bus like the other visitors?"

"Because we're special." I was done explaining. I eased Grace off my lap and stood up. "Are you ready to go on the adventure that you've been waiting for, for so long?"

"Yes! Let's go to Graceland!"

We put our jackets on, I slung the tote bag across my body and we left the room. We headed out back to the side of the hotel Sarah had mentioned when she told me what Mark did. My heart started pounding. I wasn't sure if we would find the portal, let alone what would happen to us if we did. I picked Grace up. She seemed glad for that. I walked slowly, one step at a time.

Grace was looking down at the ground. "Where is the wormhole, Mama? I don't see one."

"I'm not exactly sure, Grace, just keep your arms around me in case we find it." She hugged me tighter. I took more steps. *I am not a bad mother.*

We walked slowly around the patch of land alongside the hotel, sort of back and forth in rows like a lawnmower would do. It was a pretty isolated area and I was glad for that, or people would have wondered what in the heck we were doing. I was about three or four feet away from the wall of the building when my knee sort of gave way. I felt something familiar, a wobbly sensation like I was surfing, or losing solid ground. I held Grace tighter, my ears started popping and everything swirled. I felt dizzy and heard her say, "Mama."

And then it was over. The ground was hard again. I was on my knees and felt like I was being choked. It took a second to realize it was Grace, holding me tight around the neck. "Grace, honey," I strained. "You're choking me."

She whimpered a bit, but loosened her grip on me. "My head feels spinny."

That made me realize that what I did was affecting her too. I put her down so I could inspect her. "I'm sorry, baby. It's over now. You're ok. Do you feel ok?"

"I don't like the wiggly worm, Mama," she whined. "I don't want to do that anymore."

"The wormhole? It's alright. The wormhole just made us a little disoriented but we're fine." I sat down and patted the ground. "See? No more spinny. No more dizzy."

"No more wiggly worm." She looked around. "Where are we, Mama? Is this Graceland?"

Again, my reactions were slow. I looked around and realized we were, in fact, at Graceland! In the backyard, just outside the back porch, which was now enclosed as a den. "Yes, Grace, I do believe we're in the backyard at Graceland."

"Can we go inside?"

Could we? I wasn't sure. I hadn't planned much past this point because I was doubtful we would make it this far. Quickly, I assessed our situation. I didn't know what the date was, nor the year, nor the time. I didn't know if Elvis was home or if he'd remember me. And it would be a strange way to introduce him to Grace, just showing up at his front door.

Grace asked again about going in to the mansion. I stood up. "Not just yet. I think we're going to go for a walk first."

"Why, Mama?"

I looked at her. "Grace, please listen to me. I need you to be quiet. No more questions. I have to think about what to do." I took her by the hand. "Let's tiptoe around to the front and go down the driveway to the gate. OK? I know this may not make sense, but …" But what? Quick. Think of a place to go that has the best chance of existing in whatever time we're in. "Grace, remember when I told you about the big Peabody Hotel and the ducks that come marching out of the elevator?"

"Yes."

"Well, before we go to Graceland, I think we're going to go see the Peabody ducks."

"OK." Then, "Where is our car?"

Nowhere where we need it. "Let Mama figure things out. Let's go, quietly now."

We followed the same path the cars do to get around the mansion to the carport. I couldn't believe this was happening! What if we were spotted by someone inside? How were we going to get downtown? I hoped there would be someone at the guard house who could help.

We seemed to make it past to the front of the property without drawing any attention. As we walked down the long, beautiful driveway that I loved so much, Grace became awestruck. "Wow, Mama. It looks just like the pictures, only bigger."

"Yes. We'll have more time later and we'll see everything," I hoped. "Thanks for being a good girl. I love you, Amazing Grace."

"To infinny and beyond, Mama Llama!"

I'll never forget the look on the face of the gate guard as we walked down from the house, a mother and child. It wasn't Uncle Travis, thank goodness. Though he might not have remembered me, this was still a strange appearance to explain. "Remember what I said about being quiet, Grace," I whispered to her before we approached him.

"Good afternoon, ma'am?" he began, a question in his voice as he tried figure out where we came from.

"Good afternoon," I replied. "I wonder if you might be able to help us catch a taxi cab?"

That made him laugh. "All the way out here? I'll have to call one for you, miss. That's the only way to get one."

"Could you, please? It would be much appreciated."

"Yes, ma'am." He went into the guard house and picked up a phone. He stared at us while he made the call. Grace was being good, still holding my hand. He came back out of the guard house. "It should be just a few minutes, ma'am. They've got a driver nearby."

"Thanks so much. We'll wait outside the gate." I started to lead Grace in that direction and noticed the gates were closed. I also saw a few Elvis fans milling about beyond the gates. I turned back around to the guard.

He was already on it. "I'll open the gates for you." He hit a button in the guard house and the big musical gates began to swing inward. He came up behind us, no doubt to prevent any fans from coming on Elvis' private property. Grace was wide eyed. "Just like the pictures," she whispered to me.

We walked through the gates and found ourselves like the rest of the Elvis fans, on the outside. Grace took it all in. Before long, a yellow taxi pulled up. The driver got out and opened the back door for us. We got in. He returned to the driver's seat and asked where we were going. "The Peabody Hotel, please," I replied.

"We're going to see the ducks!" Grace added.

The cab ride wasn't different than any other, except for the scenery. While my head spun with reactions to arriving here through the wormhole and planning what to do next, I tried to estimate what year it was. The cars would have been a giveaway if I were better at recognizing older models. It looked like the 1960s, but I wasn't sure.

Like most kids on a car ride, Grace was lulled into a relaxed, droopy state. She was either going to nod off soon or take a nap when we arrived.

The driver pulled up to the front of the hotel. I paid him in cash with a generous tip, hoping that would distract him from the slight difference in appearance of my modern currency. He opened the door for us and we got out. All we had for luggage was my tote bag so we didn't need the concierge.

We entered the Peabody lobby and Grace perked up a bit. "Mama, it's so pretty!"

"Yes it is, Grace. It's beautiful." We made our way to the front desk. The staff were friendly and attentive. Grace asked the first one she saw about the ducks and we learned they had already taken their morning walk. The next walk would be at 5pm. That gave me an excuse to ask for the time, which was 2:30pm.

The front desk attendant didn't flinch when I paid cash for a room for three nights. I didn't flinch at the price: $75!

On the way to the elevators, I noticed a newspaper sitting on a table in a sitting area. "Just a second, Grace." I went over to the paper, anxious to find our place in time. The front page declared October 15, 1965. Wow. Nearly five years since the last time I was here. Where was Elvis? What was he up to? Where was my Elvis encyclopedia when I needed it!

On the elevator ride to the 9th floor, Grace yawned, which gave me the opportunity to plan at least our next couple of hours. "Grace, it's been a long day so far and the ducks are probably resting before their next walk, so we're going to do the same. We'll get comfortable in our room and take a nap before it's time to go back down to the lobby. OK?"

"OK, Mama. I'm tired anyway." That was easy.

CHAPTER 16

I've Got to Find My Baby

Grace and I settled into Room 909, which was quite elegant. The color scheme was yellow and gold. The walls were painted a golden yellow and trimmed in white. The bedspread and pillows were a thick yellow and gold stripe pattern, regally stitched. The headboard had two tall posts. All furnishings were a rich, dark wood. The upholstery on the chairs added other colors to the room—dark orange and sage green.

I propped Grace up on some pillows and let her watch a program on the local PBS station before napping. She didn't understand why there were so few channels and not much children's programming. I fibbed and told her the hotel didn't have to offer many because Memphis has a lot to do and guests don't spend much time in their rooms.

I leaned against the headboard, next to Grace. In my head was a hurricane of thoughts and questions, the most prominent one being, "Maggie, what have you done!" I successfully traveled back to Graceland again, this time with my young daughter. I flubbed my way off the property, fleeing into a cab to the Peabody and paid cash for a room. It's October 1965. Now what?!

I looked over and Grace was sound asleep. I tucked the covers around her and turned down the volume on the TV. It was time to make the call I had to make, not knowing what would happen. Would my internet research for the old Graceland phone number prove worthy? I dialed and waited.

After a couple of rings, a woman's voice answered. "Presley residence, Alberta speaking." Elvis' maid Alberta! I doubted she would remember me.

"Yes, may I please speak to Elvis Presley?" I asked, trying to sound confident.

"I'll see if he's available. Who may I say is calling?" she inquired.

"My name is Maggie Coyle," I said, wondering if Elvis would remember me. "I'm an old friend of his. I'm in town for a few days and wanted to say hello."

"I'm going to put you on hold for a minute, honey," Alberta replied. Before she did, I heard her say, "Priscilla, dear, is Elvis awake yet? He has a call from an old friend."

Priscilla! Goodness, yes. Sweet, young Priscilla is now a resident of Graceland. She moved there in March 1963. They're not engaged yet, though. Elvis will propose to Priscilla on Christmas Eve 1966. Oh, I hope I'm not getting myself into a mess!

I was on hold for a few minutes, with no idea if Elvis would take my call. My heartbeat quickened. I glanced at Grace, still asleep.

"Hello? Maggie Coyle? This must be some kind of a joke." *It was Elvis!* I was dumbstruck at the sound of his voice again. A few seconds ticked away while I tried to get my brain in gear. "Is there someone on the other end of this line? I'm gonna hang up!"

What came out of my mouth was just above a whisper. Thank goodness Grace was asleep. "Elvis, it's Maggie. Do you remember me? The girl you called Moody? It's, uh, it's been a long time and I wanted to say hello. I'm, uh, I'm here in Memphis."

"Well, I'll be damned! Maggie the Moody girl, who disappeared from Graceland without a trace! What was that, like, five years ago? Why, I ought a slam this phone down right now!" Elvis countered. "What in the hell …"

"I know, Elvis, don't be mad, please, don't be angry," I interrupted. "I can explain. It's been a long time and I'm not here to cause any trouble." I took a breath. "I'm just wondering if I could, if we could … meet sometime?"

"I don't know," Elvis answered, defiantly. My heart sank in my chest. "Good God! You know, I was really upset when you disappeared! You left without saying goodbye. You didn't leave a note or anything, so we didn't know where to look for you. Nobody was any help. I might have been worried had I not been so pissed off. You just … left me." He sounded hurt.

"I'm so sorry, Elvis. Really and truly. I'll explain," I pleaded. "If you'll let me."

"Maggie, I don't wait around for no girl," Elvis said, defensively. "I've got a real busy life with lots of people and projects." He paused for a second. "Where are you in Memphis anyway?" Curiosity may have gotten the better of him.

"I'm at the Peabody Hotel," I said. "Maybe a day or two?" I sounded unsure, which of course I was. "I'll eventually need to return home … to St. Louis."

Elvis was quiet but I could hear him breathing. Oh, how I missed him! "Maggie," he said, calmly. "I need some time to think. I wasn't expecting to hear from some blast from the past. I'll let you know."

"OK, Elvis, I understand," I replied, trying not to sound disappointed. "Like I said, I'm at the Peabody and you can call my room. It's number 909, and if I'm away, you can leave a message for me at the front desk. I'll be sure to check for messages." I paused, thinking. "You can use a code name if you want … like Jet," I said, then laughed. I was grasping at straws, that he would remember our time together.

"Jet, oh yeah, sure, Jet," Elvis said. "Ha ha." He was quiet, then, "Maggie, I have to go now." Elvis hung up.

I held the receiver a few moments, even past the beeping when the connection went dead. *Will he call me? I hope so!*

I curled myself around my little sleeping angel and tried to breathe the tension away. With thoughts of Elvis and Grace, and despite non-stop thoughts about the potentially dramatic situation I've created for all of us, I dozed off.

When I awoke, I had no idea where I was or what time it was. The clock on the nightstand said 4:29 p.m. The ducks! My brain kicked into gear. I wanted to take Grace down to the lobby to see the famous Peabody duck procession.

Gently, I stirred her to awaken. "Grace, honey, it's time to wake up from your nap … time to go see the ducks."

"Ducks, Mama," she said, in her sweet, tired voice. She rolled over toward me and I ran my fingers through her curls to soothe her awake.

"That's right, baby. Let's get ourselves out of this bed and down to the lobby." We freshened up a bit and left the room.

Just in time, we arrived in the lobby for the 5 o'clock Peabody Duck March. As a prelude, the host told us how the tradition began in the 1930s when the general manager and his friend put three of their live duck decoys into the Peabody fountain. "It was meant to be a prank, but was very well received," he told the crowd gathered. A few years later, a former circus animal trainer offered to bring the ducks to the fountain each day. He even taught them to march. "Mr. Pembroke was the Peabody Duck master for 50 years!"

The host told us that the ducks live in a Royal Duck Palace on the roof of the hotel. "Their marble and glass home includes a fountain, a front yard and a small house and that looks like a mini Peabody Hotel."

"The ducks are living it up like we are," the man next to me said.

The host called our attention to the elevator. Soon, a bell announced its arrival and the doors opened to reveal five ducks. "Mama! They're so cute!" Grace exclaimed.

I laughed at the sight. "They sure are."

One by one, the ducks waddled—or marched—across the red carpet to the beautiful fountain. Folks applauded. "Ladies and gentleman, these are five North American mallards, one male with the white collar and green head, and four hens. The lady ducks may not be as colorful, but we assure you, that's only when it comes to feathers," he joked. The crowd laughed.

I helped Grace work her way up to the front where some other children had the best view as the ducks plopped themselves into the fountain and swam around. Tourist camera bulbs were flashing to capture the moment. I found myself standing next to our host. "How long are these ducks on assignment?" I asked.

"Several weeks only," he replied. "We have a local farmer who gives us a team of wild ducks every three months. Our Duck master trains them and teaches them to march, then they get to retire back to the farm."

"How wonderful."

"Mama, I wanna take one of those ducks home with me!" Grace said, running up to me. "I could teach him how to walk out of our house and we could get a red carpet for the front porch and I could invite people over and put on a show! Could we make a little pond in our front yard, too?" She was so imaginative.

"I think these ducks are happy enough to live here at the Peabody with their family so I don't think we'll take one of them away," I responded. "Would you settle for a new stuffed duck for your tea parties at home?"

"Yes! Where can we get one?" Grace looked around the lobby.

"I'm guessing in the gift shop," I said, reaching for my purse and realizing I didn't bring it with me. "But you know what? I didn't bring any money down here. We'll have to go back to the room."

While I said that, Grace made a beeline for the concierge. I hurried to catch up with her. "Grace! You shouldn't wander away from me like that!" I exclaimed, then remembered it's 1965. Probably not as big of a worry.

"Mama, this is Robert, and he says they have ducks for kids in the gift shop. And, he said I can stay with him and watch the ducks swim in the fountain while you go upstairs and get some money." Grace had it all figured out.

I looked at Robert inquisitively. "Are you sure? We don't want to be a bother."

"Watching the ducks with our guests is part of the job, ma'am," Robert said. "No problem at all. I'd be happy to spend a few minutes with this little lady."

"Grace Christina Coyle," Grace added, taking Robert by the hand. "It's very nice to meet you."

I took the elevator to our floor and smiled as I headed down the hallway to our room. Grace is such a breath of fresh air, even a hotel concierge gets taken in by her bubbly charm.

Inside the room, I grabbed my wallet and decided to use the restroom before heading back down. While the toilet was flushing, I thought I heard a knock on the door. I quickly washed my hands and heard another knock as I came out of the bathroom. Grace is back already. I hope she didn't convince Robert to buy her a duck!

I opened the door and had to grab it to support myself when I saw who it was. *Elvis!* I sucked air. I could not believe it.

"Elvis! My goodness! I didn't know you were coming! Did I, did I miss a call? Oh my gosh, I'm sorry if I did! I was down in the lobby with Gr … with the other guests, watching the ducks. You know, they're so remarkable, the way they …" Here I was, making a fool of myself in front of the King of Rock 'n Roll—again. I stopped myself from babbling. I sighed, smiled and gazed at him. He looked terribly handsome in black jeans and black jean jacket, with a yellow shirt with the collar up and out. His jacket had accent piping like mine but was more western looking.

Elvis smiled back. "It *is* you. Are you gonna let me in?" He cocked his head to the side and looked at me with those beautiful blue eyes.

"Yes! Of course. Come in," I said, opening the door and taking a few steps back into the room. As I did, and Elvis entered, it was then that I was stunned by who followed him into the room. Red West. I gasped. The guy who had it in for me last time was now standing in my hotel room.

"Hello, Red," I said, as casually as possible. "How are you? How are both of you? Please, have a seat." I looked around and was glad there were two chairs with a side table in front of the window. Red went quietly to one chair and said down. "Hello, Maggie," he mustered.

Elvis was still standing, so I did the same. He was really checking me out. I guess I looked different to him. After all, I was about five years older than the last time he saw me. Our eyes met and I couldn't help it, I broke into a big smile. Which means those two indentations in my cheeks were showing.

"There they are," Elvis said, smiling. "Those dimples. Goddamn, Moody, it *is* you!" With that, he reached for me and enveloped me in a big hug. I hugged him back, forgetting that Red was in the room. We stayed in our embrace for several seconds; I could have stayed forever. Then Elvis released me, grabbing my upper arms. "What the hell's going on? Why are you back after all this time? Calling me and getting me curious enough to drive down here!" He was a little feisty.

"Thank you. So much. For coming, Elvis." I said. "If I'd have known, I'd be a little more presentable. I'm a bit casual now, not made up or anything."

"Forget about that," Elvis said. "But you need to answer some questions."

"I know," I agreed. "I do. And I intend to. Please. Have a seat. Can I get you anything? Should I call room service?" *Oh shit. Grace. She's downstairs with the concierge. What should I do? How much time do I have before they come looking for me?*

"Nah, I'm fine," Elvis replied. "In fact, Red can run and get us something." While I fretted about Grace, Elvis directed his attention to Red. "Hey, Red, why don't you go get some sodas and snacks for the room. Give us a little time to talk, OK?"

"Sure, Elvis," Red replied, getting up and heading toward the door. When he passed me, he nodded at me and simply said, "Maggie." Then he was gone.

Elvis took one of the chairs. I chose to sit on the bed across from him. He was fidgety as usual. He leaned toward me, elbows on his knees, giving me a serious look. "Spill it," he said. "I wanna know where you went and why the hell you left me."

CHAPTER 17

Heartbreak Hotel

It was good to gaze once again at the oh-so-handsome King of Rock 'n Roll. Those blue eyes were smoldering and Elvis was his usual "shaky leg" self. I put my daydreaming on pause to give him the explanation he demanded.

"Elvis," I began. "Do you remember the night we sat on your bed in Graceland and I told you I was from St. Louis and traveled to Memphis, and partied on Beale Street with a friend and woke up the next day in your storage closet in your basement?"

"I thought I forgot such crazy talk, but now that you mention it," he replied, then laughed at me. Déjà vu.

"That's right, you laughed at me," I continued. "But it was the truth, Elvis. I came from your basement … and from somewhere else." I closed my eyes for a second and reopened them, meeting his. "I came from the future. I had traveled to the past when I met you." Our eyes were still locked on one another.

"That's bull crap!" he exclaimed. "Don't tell me you're just as nutty as you were last time. C'mon, girl."

"I know it sounds ridiculous and impossible," I said. "It does for me, too. But you've heard of time travel, haven't you?"

"Maybe at the movies or on TV," Elvis said. "That stuff's just science fiction."

"I thought so too, Elvis," I added. "Then it became real for me. I've been trying to get back to you since the first time."

Elvis was quiet. He shifted around in his seat. He switched to wiggling the other leg incessantly. He shook his head.

"Moody, I liked you. You were different than the other girls. We connected, and it was fun having you around," he paused. "You left me." Elvis actually looked hurt, and I started wondering why I ever thought this visit was a good idea. "Why would you do that and come back years later with this bullshit story? Can't you just tell me the truth?" Elvis asked.

I was quiet. Elvis continued. "Were you married? Did you go back to St. Louis to some husband?" he implored.

"I was born in 1977," I said, emphatically. *There, I said it.* I looked Elvis in the eyes. "Now, if we want to skip over the science fiction, that's fine. There is more I can tell you. Other than the science fiction."

Elvis leaned back in the chair, the fingers of one hand fiddling with the ring he was wearing on the other. "You do know it's just 1965, right, Moody? Hell, 1977 is 12 years away and you're, what, 30-something now? You're awful at math!"

I had to smile. I couldn't expect anyone to rationalize what has happened to me. I continued. "I went back to St. Louis with my reporter friend I had traveled to Memphis with and we became a couple. His name is Chris. We live together in St. Louis. We've been together for about five years."

Again, Elvis was quiet. There was a sudden knock on the door that made both of us jump. *Grace! Oh no, this is not going as I imagined!* I got off the bed quickly to head to the door but Elvis grabbed me by the wrist.

"OK, so you have a boyfriend and I have a girlfriend. Big deal. Why come back to Memphis to tell me that?" he asked.

I closed my eyes, breathed in and out, and replied, "Just a minute." I walked to the door and opened it.

"Mama! Mama! I got a duck!" Grace said excitedly as she ran into my arms. "Robert said it was OK, the gift shop can charge our room for it!" she paused. "Is it OK, Mama?" Robert was standing, grinning, just outside the doorway.

"Of course," I said, giving her a hug. "Thank you, Robert. I'm sorry I was detained," I added, wondering if he could see past me to my guest. "Thank you so much for taking care of Grace."

If he did spot Elvis, he didn't say anything. "My pleasure, ma'am. That's quite a young lady you've got there. Enjoy your stay at the Peabody." Tipping his cap, he turned and departed down the hallway.

Grace bounded into the room while I was closing the door and yelled, "Mama!" She ran back to me, grabbing me around the legs. My little girl had seen Elvis Presley for the first time. Elvis had stopped fidgeting and sat frozen in his seat.

"Mama, that man looks like Elvis Presley!" Grace said to me, trying to lower her voice.

"Grace, that man *is* Elvis Presley," I replied, untangling myself from her pint-sized bear hug.

"But you said he went up to H--," Grace whispered, eyes wide.

"Never mind," I interrupted quickly and took her by the hand. "Grace, I'd like to introduce you to the one and only Elvis Presley. Elvis, this is Grace." My heart was beating so hard it could have flopped out of my chest onto the hotel bed.

Elvis was the first to speak. He extended his hand to Grace and said, "It's mighty nice to meet you, Grace."

His hand still outstretched to her, Grace took a shy step forward. Shifting her new duck to her left hand, she put her right in his. "I'm Grace Christina Coyle," she said quietly, sweetly. "And you're Elvis Presley."

Elvis laughed. I exhaled. "Yes, I am. From head to toe!" Grace giggled. "What's that you've got there in your arms, a Peabody duck?" he asked her. As Grace answered him, there was another knock on the door. My hand went to my heart. Who would it be this time? Sensing my confusion, Elvis said, "That's probably Red."

"I'll get it," I said as I headed back to the door. Grace had begun to tell Elvis about the ducks and their performance in the lobby.

It was Red and his arms were full of drinks and snacks. "Hey, Red, c'mon in," I said. "Do you need some help?"

"I got it," he replied, heading past me into the room. Red started setting the items on the dresser, noticing Grace with Elvis. He reached for the ice bucket and looked directly at me.

"Grace," I said, motioning her toward Red and me. "This is Elvis' friend and bodyguard, Red West."

Grace extended her hand to him, more quickly this time. "Your name is Red?" she exclaimed. "And you're a bodyguard?"

Red smiled and shook hands with Grace. "Nice to meet you, little lady," he said. He gave me another look. "I'm going to get ice."

"Can I go? I wanna push the button that makes the ice come out!" Grace said. Her enthusiasm for the little things in life was boundless.

Red looked at Elvis. Elvis nodded slightly. "C'mon, Grace, let's go find the ice maker," Red said. Fearlessly, Grace headed out of the room with the bodyguard she just met. As the door closed, I heard her say, "Did your parents name you Red because you have red hair?"

I turned to Elvis. His hand covered his mouth and he was staring at me, such a serious look disrupting his beautiful face. "Maggie," he said softly.

I rushed to him, kneeling on the floor at his feet. "Elvis," I replied. He called me Maggie instead of Moody.

"Maggie," he began again, and closed his eyes. When he opened them, I swore I saw tears forming. My heart broke a little. I put my hands on his knees. "Is she," he started to ask. "Is Grace," he tried again but stopped, dropping his head into both hands, bringing his elbows to his knees.

"I don't know, Elvis," I replied, rubbing his arms and answering the unfinished question. "I'm not sure. I don't want to hurt you. I just … thought you should meet her. She's so amazing. I'm sorry. Maybe this was a bad idea. Oh, Elvis, I don't know what to do!"

There was a knock on the door. Red and Grace were back. Not wanting to leave Elvis' side, I reluctantly got up and went to let them in. Grace was her usual, bouncy self. Elvis recomposed himself and made eye contact with Red. Touching his fingers to his temples, he communicated some sort of signal with Red. Red nodded. Elvis stood up, shook his head back and forth, as if dusting off a bad memory.

"How about we have a sing along!" Grace suggested. I love my girl for her ability to keep things on the sunny side.

"Sorry, Grace, but I have to go now," Elvis said to her. "Maybe some other time?" My heart was breaking a little, again.

"OK," she replied to him. "When you're Elvis Presley, you probably have a lot of stuff to do. To me, she asked, "Can I turn on the TV, Mama?"

"Sure, Grace," I replied. Red was already opening the door and Elvis was headed that way. "But first please say goodbye to our guests."

"Bye, Elvis! Bye, Red! See you later," Grace said, waving goodbye then running to the TV to flip the dial in search of something to watch.

I headed toward the door after Elvis. Reaching for his hand, I said, "Elvis, can we … I'm sorry. Thanks so much for the surprise visit. It was wonderful to see you again. You look great."

"Not right now, Maggie," the King of Rock 'n Roll answered. "I gotta go." With that, the door closed and he was gone.

I burst into tears, but for the sake of my daughter, sucked them back in. I swallowed hard and clenched my teeth as I prepared a snack for Grace while she watched TV. I sat on the bed behind her, my back on the pillows and headboard. Quietly, I cried.

What have I done.

CHAPTER 18

Edge of Reality

When I cry, I become a snotty mess, especially when trying to hold it in. Grace was mostly oblivious to my emotional reaction to Elvis' leaving until I blew my nose for the third time.

"Mama, are you getting sick?" she asked, crawling across the bed toward me. Grace did something so sweet; she took my face in her little hands. "You're blowing your nose and your eyes are all red."

"I'm fine, baby," I replied. "I've just got a headache; maybe my sinuses are acting up again."

"Please feel better, Mama," she pleaded. "I like Memphis and I like Elvis. I hope we can stay for a while and do more fun things!"

"I will. And we will," I reassured her. "I'm going to go get a cold wash rag for my face. How about you watch a little more TV, or maybe get out the coloring book and crayons they gave you."

"OK, Mama." She went back to her entertainment.

I went into the bathroom and looked at myself in the mirror: a puffy fright. My nose was stopped up and my head was aching behind my eyebrows. I splashed warm water on my face. Them I soaked a wash rag in cold water and covered my face with it. I breathed deeply, allowing my emotions to subside. It was going to be OK. I have to stay level-headed. Keep my wits about me. My heart cannot rule my head.

While I had this silent pep talk with myself, there was a knock at the door. Now what? I went to the door and opened it, and there was no one in the hallway. Strange. I heard the knock again, and this time I realized it came from behind me, from the door near the dresser that led to an adjoining room. That got Grace's attention.

"Who is it, Mama?" she asked.

I looked at her and wanted to know the same. "Yes? Who's there?" I said somewhat timidly at the adjoining door.

"Maggie, it's me, Red. Can I come in?" the voice said, in a whisper. Red West? How in the … I turned the knob and opened the door, which revealed another open door and Red West. Behind him, the room was dark.

"Hey," he said, quietly. He looked back into the dark room then at me. "OK if I come in?"

"Sure," I replied hesitantly, because this new Red West was hard to get used to, not threatening or harassing me.

Red entered our room, closing his room door behind him quietly. I closed our adjoining door and eyed him curiously. Grace's eyes had lit up. "Hello, Red West! Are you here to be our bodyguard, too?"

"If you need guarding, I'm your guy," he responded. "Right now, I need to talk to your mom for a few minutes."

"Of course," she replied. "I'm coloring. Can I color something for you, Red?"

"That'd be mighty fine," he said.

"Grace, honey, why don't you color on the bed," I suggested. "Red and I need to sit at the table and chairs."

"OK." Looking at Red, she added, "You're going to love this," pointing to her coloring.

"I'm sure I will," Red said with a grin. Grace's enthusiasm was contagious.

Red and I went sat in the chairs, facing each other. I began in a hushed tone. "Why did you come from the next room? Is Elvis alright?"

Red nodded. "Yeah. He's in the next room, with a headache. Gets 'em when he's angry or upset." He paused. I realized my jaw had dropped open and closed it. Red continued. "When he gave me the signal earlier, I was prepared to get him out of the hotel and back to Graceland. When we got down to the lobby, he told me to get the room next to yours. So I did. He's lying in there in the dark, but I doubt he's sleeping."

I closed my eyes. "Red," I began.

"You know, Maggie, I just don't get it." He was practicing some restraint but I could tell he was aggravated.

"Red," I began again. "I can explain." *Here I go, explaining again.* He was quiet. Grace's TV show filled the silence. "I know it's your job to protect Elvis. To keep him safe, to prevent him from getting hurt. You weren't fair to me the last time, but I understand you were just doing your job."

"That was years ago!" he said with all the force a blunt whisper could muster. "And you disappeared! Elvis was upset. He was seriously pissed. Who do you think he took it out on? Me! His bodyguard. At first, he thought I let your disappearance happen because I didn't like you, so he lectured me. Then, after I helped him search around for you, he thought I had something to do with you leaving Graceland, so he blamed me."

"I'm sorry," I replied, hanging my head. "Let me tell you what happened." I met his eyes. "Just listen. You're going to be inclined not to believe me but I promise I'm telling you the truth."

Red let out a heavy sigh and sat back in his chair. "Go ahead. This better be good, not the nonsense from last time."

I sighed, too. "I probably seemed like any other girl back then, trying to meet Elvis and spend time with him. For me, it was truly a dream come true because I loved him my whole life." Red rolled his eyes. I continued. "I was born the day he …" I stopped. Do I go there now?

"The day he what?" Red asked, annoyed.

"I'll get back to that," I said, changing my mind about my approach. "Elvis and I had a wonderful connection. He was kind to let me stay a few days. I'm not stupid, Red. I know about Anita, and Priscilla. I know there are lots of girls. But he made me feel special and I was scared, and at the same time just living in the moment."

"Scared of what … Elvis?" Red's eyebrows furrowed.

"Scared of my circumstances, of how I arrived at Graceland. How I woke up in the little room in the basement."

Red harrumphed. "From what I remember, you just make it up as you go, don't you?"

"I'm going to tell you where I came from and when I do, you'll understand why I had to leave. I had to go back."

"Go back where?" He was getting impatient.

Here goes. "Red, when I traveled from St. Louis to Memphis, I was bringing a reporter on a behind-the-scenes tour of Graceland." That raised an eyebrow. I continued. "For a newspaper story. In 2006. I came from 2006, Red. I came from the future. I was born the day Elvis ..." Red's guffaw stopped me in mid-sentence. It even got Grace's attention.

"What's so funny, Mama?"

Red continued laughing and shook his head.

"Never mind, Grace," I answered her. "I'm just telling Red a story. You're being a very good girl and I appreciate that. Give us a few more minutes, please."

"OK, Mama," she replied. "But if you start telling jokes, I wanna tell some, too."

I was able to meet Red's eyes and we held our gaze for a few seconds. "Red, I know it seems impossible to comprehend. Believe me, I've been through a lot with this." For emphasis, I slowly glanced at Grace and back at him. "A lot." I paused, gathering my best words. Red apparently got my implication and dropped his head into one hand. "I had to go back and figure out what happened, how it was possible to start the day in 2006 and wake up in 1960." Red looked back at me. "It was wrong to leave Elvis the way I did, but I was afraid and needed some answers." Another pause. "Red, I was born the day he died." That got his attention and he locked me in a cold stare. "Elvis died on August 16, 1977, the same day I was born."

No matter how many times I'd made this statement, it always carried hurt along with it. This time, my heart broke again and I lost it, bursting into tears. Forgetting him, forgetting Grace. Terribly sad for the bomb I just dropped, one Red West may not even believe.

"Mama!" Grace scrambled to my side. "What's the matter? Why are you crying? Red West, what's wrong?" She put her arms around me. "Mama, Mama," she comforted me.

Red did the gentlemanly thing and handed me his handkerchief from his pocket. I wiped my eyes. "Grace, honey, would you please bring Mama some tissues from the bathroom?" She jumped off the bed and ran to fetch them.

I used the moment to try to connect with Red again. He looked terribly conflicted. On one hand, I think he wanted to tell me I was crazy. On the other, he was shocked into silence by my revelation. He leaned forward in his chair, hands folded, arms resting on his legs. "What can I say, Maggie? You got me. I'm speechless. Never in my life could I have predicted this—from you or any girl. Why go to the trouble? Why make up such awful lies?"

Grace returned with half a tissue box in each hand. I took them from her and she sat next to me on the bed, gazing up with concern. I blew my nose, caressed the top of her head and put my arm around her. I looked back at Red. "Proof. I'll show you proof. Proof that what I said is true. If I do that, then you'll have no choice but to believe me."

There was a noise at the adjoining doors. We all swung our heads in that direction as Elvis stepped into the room, covering his eyes with a hand while they adjusted to the light.

"Elvis!" Grace squealed, heading toward him. "I didn't know you were here! I would have watched TV with you while Mama talked to Red West." When she reached him, she hesitated briefly, then held out her arms. Elvis scooped her up, his eyes dashing back and forth between Red and me while he did so.

"Adults talk too much," he said to Grace, but with a smoldering side-glance at us. "They talk too much and it's boring."

"I don't know what they were talking about but it made Mama

cry," she said with all seriousness, gazing at him since they were at eye level.

"You don't say," Elvis responded. "Well, I'm sure it's nothing for you to worry about, Little One." Again, when he looked at us his eyes flashed a pulse of anger. "My headache is better," he continued, looking back at Grace. "What do you say we go and do something fun?" Elvis tickled her.

"Yippee!" Grace exclaimed, giggling, too. "I love to do fun things! Let's all go have some fun, Mama! You, too, Red West!" She was thrilled.

Red and I got up and followed Elvis and Grace toward to door. I grabbed my purse and stepped in the bathroom to check my face and wipe away the remaining tears. Elvis put Grace down and she hopped out into the hallway. Turning back to us, he pointed two fingers and said, "You two, to be continued."

CHAPTER 19

Take Me to the Fair

"Let's go to the Fairgrounds," Elvis said, and just as I remembered, his world sprang into action—first Red with some phone calls from the hotel lobby, then his team as they produced the latest concoction of Elvis' spontaneous desires. Even though it would be dark by the time we arrived, we were going to get private, late-night access to Memphis' main attraction: Fairgrounds Amusement Park.

"What's at the Fairgrounds at nighttime?" Grace asked from the back seat of Elvis' black Cadillac, sitting next to Red. Elvis had insisted I ride up front with him.

"The Pippin!" Elvis exclaimed, glancing back at her.

"The Pippin? What's a Pippin?"

"It's a roller coaster. Wait until you see this wooden racetrack. We're gonna ride it as many times as we want!"

"Yay!" Grace bounced on the seat.

I had to be the voice of reason. "Grace, a roller coaster sounds like a ride for adults so we'll have to see about you riding it. It may not be safe."

"Aw, no fair!

Elvis caught my drift. "Your mama's right. We also have the Grand Carousel and we can ride it a bunch of times."

"A carrot sell?"

"Ha! It's a big 'ole merry-go-round with giant horses," he answered. "You can ride a different horse each time."

"I love merry-go-rounds!" She got serious for a moment. "I hope we can find it in the dark."

Elvis laughed again. To me, he said, "You only gave her one of your dimples?"

He drove the four of us to the Fairgrounds in midtown Memphis. I didn't know much, except it had been around for a long time and was closed, in my time. It had been renamed Libertyland and I remember reading that the Zippin Pippin, Elvis' favorite roller coaster, was sold to another amusement park up north.

When we arrived at the entrance, a couple of security guards were waiting to let us in, as well as several more cars containing the rest of Elvis' group. The sign at the entrance read: "Mid-South Fair, since 1912." I hoped the rides weren't that old!

We parked in a row and rolled out of the cars. Elvis introduced us to the group, which included his foreman, Marty Lacker; assistants Joe Esposito and Richard Davis; his cousin Billy Smith; Red's cousin, Sonny West; Army buddy Charlie Hodge; Jerry Schilling and his friend, Mike Keeton; plus a bunch of girls. I scanned the group for Priscilla but didn't see her. I wondered if Elvis made her stay home.

"Maggie and Grace haven't been to our fairgrounds," Elvis told the group. "Let's show 'em what we got!"

"Yeah, let's go ride the Pippin!" shouted Sonny. Such a handsome guy—tall, with a great smile. I doubted he remembered me,

"Not so fast," Elvis directed. "We're gonna start at the merry-go-round, so Grace can ride the horses." There were a few groans but the group headed toward the Grand Carousel.

And Grand it was, with big, beautiful, hand-carved horses. I'm sure they fetched a fair price when the carousel came down. Grace took one look at them and ran for the entrance. "Slow down, honey! Be careful!" I sounded like every mom at a theme park.

"She'll be alright," Elvis said, winking at me. "I'll keep my eye on her." I think the King was warming to my girl.

When we boarded the ride, most folks climbed up and picked out their horses, but some of the guys acted macho, like it was too sissy for them. Red and Sonny stayed back and lit up cigarettes, no doubt in a ruse to avoid the ride. The ladies were all in, and the smart guys followed them to ride alongside.

Grace chose a pink horse. Elvis got to where she was before I did and hoisted her up and held her in place. My mind immediately flashed to the scene in *Change of Habit,* with Elvis, Mary Tyler Moore and the little girl on a merry-go-round. It was one of my favorite movies and I smiled knowing it was about four years from being released.

"What are you smiling about, Moody?" Elvis asked. He said my nickname.

"Just having a happy," I replied. He wouldn't get the joke referring to the movie song.

"Why don't you have a happy on this horse?" he said, motioning to a sassy green horse next to Grace's.

"Don't mind if I do." I put my foot in the stirrups to boost myself up. Next thing I knew his hands were on my butt, giving me a lift. I gave him a look. "Thanks for the boost."

It wasn't long before the ride attendant started up the music and we began going around, and up and down. Grace squealed with delight. She's never been on a big carousel, just little ones at school picnics and kiddie lands.

Elvis was standing between us, closer to her, ensuring she didn't wiggle around and fall off. His other hand was on my stirrups, and occasionally rubbed my calf. *Yowsa.* "You like this, Grace?" he asked her.

"Oh, yes! We're really going up and down!" That made him laugh, which was music to my ears.

Our extended ride was not adventurous, so I wasn't surprised when Elvis started looking for mischief. To the extent that they could see each other in the round, the guys were poking fun, exaggerating the up and down movement of the horses to the amusement of the girls.

"Look at Billy," Elvis yelled to the group. "He's riding that horse like it's his first time!" He cracked up and so did everyone else.

"This ain't my first rodeo," Billy yelled back.

"She's better lookin' than your last girlfriend!" said Joe. More laughs.

I could tell I had limited time before Elvis wandered away. "Why don't you help me down and I'll stand by Grace?"

"Why don't you get off your high horse?" Elvis quipped, helping me climb off. When I had both feet on the ground, our bodies were very close together. I could smell his scent and feel his heat.

"I doubt we're supposed to be moving around while the ride is in motion," I said softly.

"You'd better stop moving then, or I'll throw a saddle on you," he whispered back. My heart thudded in my chest. I tried to recover by backing up to Grace's side, her pink horse hypnotically going up and down. My eyes remained with his.

Someone yelloing broke our lustful gaze. Richard's horse was malfunctioning. "Look at Richard … his 'get up and go' got up and went!"

"No bucking that bronco!" Jerry said. The group busted out laughing.

Elvis left in search of the jokers. He turned back to us and said, "I'll be back." I smiled at the *Spinout* song reference, another movie song he hadn't recorded yet!

When the group tired of the rhythmic repetition of the carousel horses, Marty signaled the attendant and the ride slowed to an end. Sonny yelled to the group from the grounds, "Let's go get that Pippin pumpin'!"

A chorus of agreement followed. The group left the Grand Carousel in search of the Pippin roller coaster. Grace and I followed them, walking hand in hand. "Do I get to ride the Pippin, Mama?"

"We'll see, Grace. I need to find out if it's safe for kids."

"Maybe they have a kiddie land, Mama, with rides for me."

Elvis heard that, somehow, and turned back to us. "They sure do, Grace, and I promise we'll go check it out after we ride the roller coaster." To Joe, he said, "Find one of the carnies and have him fire up the kiddie section."

I took one look at the Pippin and made a parental decision: no for Grace. She took it well; I've taught her that being in a group means taking turns.

Most of the group had run ahead and was climbing into their seats on the ride. Elvis turned around and said, "C'mon, Maggie, you're riding with me." I shook my head and nodded toward Grace so he would realize I couldn't go. "Oh, yeah, right. Well, you two stay right there and watch." He turned around and jogged toward the Pippin entrance.

Grace and I found a nearby bench with a decent view. Before Elvis climbed in to his seat, he yelled out to us. "Maggie! After a few times around, I'll find a babysitter so you can ride!"

"OK!" I yelled back, also giving him the "OK" sign.

"I'm not a baby," Grace said, with dramatic emphasis.

"Of course you're not," I responded, putting my arm around her. "Elvis didn't mean anything by that. He's just having fun with his friends."

"I wish I could ride the Pippin," she said with a pout.

"Grace!" I jiggled her. "We're at a theme park and you don't have a smile on your face?" I took her chin my hand. "You don't want the smile police to find you, do you?"

"Mama, there's no such thing as smile police." That made her smile. "And anyway, it's dark and this is a private party."

"Alright then, let's party!"

The sounds of shouting, howling and laughter pulled our attention as the Pippin descended its first hill, Elvis leading the way, riding solo in the first car, his hands in the air. Despite the night, Grace and I could see enough to follow the train cars on the wooden track. It looked like a pretty simple ride to me, although I have the benefit of knowing the "daredevil" roller coasters of the future.

The ride didn't last that long, about a minute, and we could hear the train come to a stop. It started up again soon after, the sound of the chains on the tracks kicking in, pulling them up the first hill for round two.

The group rode the Pippin four times, filling the air each time with the sounds of thrills. At one point, I noticed that Elvis had given up the front car and taken the rear. I've always thought that was the car to ride in, because you can feel it lift off the tracks.

Grace had crawled on to my lap to snuggle a bit. She was being good; this had to be hard for a child to understand. "Can we go to kiddie land soon?" she asked.

"Yes, honey, soon."

After the fourth ride came to a halt, it didn't start back up again. Soon, we noticed Red making his way toward us. I laughed. "Did you pull the short straw, Red?"

He stopped in front of us on the bench. "Actually, I did not. I get the pleasure of escorting Miss Grace to kiddie land, while you go ride the Pippin." At that, Grace jumped off my lap and scurried over to take Red by the hand.

"I don't have to ride the Pippin, Red. We can both take Grace to kiddie land."

Just then I heard Elvis shouting from the Pippin. "C'mon, Maggie, get your butt up here, it's your turn!"

Looking at me, Red motioned toward the ride. "What Elvis wants, Elvis gets." I couldn't disagree.

"Be careful. Both of you," I said, before walking away. "I'll join you soon."

As I headed toward the Pippin, I heard Grace say to Red, "When I grow up, it's gonna be 'What Grace wants, Grace gets.'" Red laughed.

When I arrived up on the boarding deck, the group was as wound up as ever. Elvis was still in the back seat of the back car, and had scooted over to make room for me. "C'mere, woman," he said. That was all the encouragement I needed to climb in. The ride started up and I put both hands on the handlebar in front of me. "What are ya, chicken?" Elvis asked.

"No, but you got a head start on me. I need to see what I'm up against before I go free handed."

He scooted closer to me. "What you're up against, Moody, is me." He kissed me on the ear.

We rode the Pippin three times. There was hootin' and hollerin' from every car. I screamed, and laughed until my stomach hurt. There really isn't anything like a roller coaster ride to make you forget about everything else. The Pippin was a good one, too—plenty of speed and turns and hills—considering its place in time.

When we pulled into the station after the third time around, I'd had enough. I wondered how Elvis and his friends could go this many times. "Elvis, I'm done. That was fun. But I need to go find Grace and make sure she hasn't run Red ragged."

Elvis yelled a command to the ride operator. "That's all for now!" To his entourage, he said, "Let's go folks. We're movin' on." As the guys and girls climbed out of the cars, I couldn't help but notice that some of them seemed relieved.

"Where to, boss?" Mike asked, as we left the Pippin.

"Why don't you head to Noah's Ark," he suggested. I saw a couple of the girls look at each other and roll their eyes. "I'm gonna walk Maggie over to kiddie land."

The group headed one way, Elvis and me another. "What kind of ride is Noah's Ark?" I asked.

"It's a fun house," he replied. "There's this hilarious part where an air hose blows up out of the ground. When the girls walk over it, their dresses blow up, especially if it's their first time!" He laughed. "It's even funny when they know it's coming, watching them try to hold their dresses down."

"Is it a house or an ark?"

"It's an ark, with animals and Noah, like in the Bible, plus lots of gags."

"I don't remember *gags* from the Bible."

"What are you worried about, woman? You're wearing pants."

It was strange, walking through an amusement park in the dark. Elvis took my hand. I wasn't worried—who could see—but Chris dashed through my mind. When we got to the kiddie land, it wasn't hard to spot Grace and Red because there was only one ride running, with cute little racecars going around in a circle. Grace was beeping her car horn continuously. Red was waving to her each time she passed him. The ride operator looked half asleep.

I let go of Elvis' hand before they saw us and approached Red. "Thanks," I said. "For entertaining Grace."

"Not a problem at all," he replied. "She's a good kid."

"Why aren't you on there with her, Red?" Elvis joked. "I'd like to see your big ole butt crammed into one of those cars." He laughed.

Red laughed, too. "I believe that would slow things down a bit."

"Mama! Elvis!" Grace yelled from the ride, then beeped her horn some more. We waved, and continued to do so when she passed. Eventually, the ride operator slowed it down to a stop. He went over to Grace and carefully lifted her out of the car and down from the ride. She scrambled over to us.

"I've been on three rides already and they let me stay on extra-long!" She went up to Elvis and threw her arms around his legs in a big bear hug. "Thank you, Elvis. This is so much fun."

"You're welcome, Gracie." He looked around kiddie land. "What else is there to do around here?"

"Well, I still need to ride the Ferris wheel. Will you ride with me, Mama?"

"Of course." We headed to the little Ferris wheel and the ride operator followed us.

Grace looked back at Elvis and Red. "You can ride, too, but I don't think you can sit in the same car. It's just not big enough, 'cause it's for little kids."

They both smiled. I knew Elvis was itching to be with his friends and ride the adult rides. "Elvis, we can rejoin you all after this. Just let me know where to find you."

He jumped on it. "Yeah, that sounds like a good idea, Maggie." Turning to Red, "Let's go round everybody up and ride the Whip." Back to me, "Ask that operator to point you to the Whip and we'll meet up there in a little bit."

"Sounds like a plan," I replied.

As Grace and I went 'round in the mini Ferris wheel, she asked, "What's the Whip, Mama?" Will I be too little for that, too?"

"We'll see, Grace. I need to check it out when we get there."

"OK." She paused. "I'm having a good time, Mama, don't worry. Even if I don't get to go on all of the rides."

I hugged her closer to me. "You are a sweet one, Grace Christina. I love you."

"I love YOU, Mama!" She put her hand on top of mine. "I think I love Elvis, too." *You and me, both.*

When the ride ended, we got off and followed the directions to get to the Whip. It wasn't very far away and we heard the fun before we got there.

The Whip ride reminded me of the Scrambler from school picnics growing up. We loved going on that to squish each other as the ride sped up and jerked us around.

Grace and I walked up to the rail where we could watch them ride. Sure enough, there was a whole lot of squishing going on. The cars went around the track, and whipped around the corners, sending riders to the sides of the cars, and into each other. Elvis, of course, was one of the "squooshers." He spotted us and yelled, "Hey! Let's stop for a second so we can board some new riders!"

Grace didn't miss a beat. "Do I get to ride the Whip, Mama?"

"Well …" I watched the ride slow down. "I think so, but let's make sure you're on the side that doesn't get squished. You're a little small for that."

"Yes, yes!" she squealed. "I wanna be the squoosher!"

Elvis gave a few orders and moved some people around on the ride to make room for us. He was standing by an empty car. "Come here, Gracie, let me get you up into this one." He lifted her up and set her on the side I was hoping for, to be safe. "And you," he extended his hand to me. "Get in." I climbed up and sat in the middle. "Nope. Move over." He motioned to the left, that cocky grin on his face.

"But …" I stalled. It was too late. He climbed into the car and plopped down in the middle, between us.

"Yeah, yeah! Mama's gonna get squooshed!" Grace giggled.

"Yes, she is," Elvis added. Grace laughed harder.

The ride fired up and we started making our way down the track. When we got to the first corner, the ride made a move like a slingshot and whipped us toward my end of the car. Grace whipped into Elvis and Elvis whipped into me, with a little extra shove from that pelvis of his. I was squished, but couldn't help but laugh. And scream.

The three of us, along with the rest of the riders, laughed and yelled the whole time. After several minutes, Elvis gave a signal and the ride started to slow down. Grace was cracking up. "Mama, we sure did squoosh you good!"

"Yeah, we did!" Elvis added.

I let out a big sigh. "Now I know why this ride is called the Whip!" I was pooped, actually, and my sigh gave way to a yawn.

Elvis spotted it. "Guys," he addressed the group. "Let's wind things down a bit over at Lover's Lane." That was met with animal growls and wolf calls. I imagined several couples were going to have a good time.

"Lover's Lane," Grace chimed in. "What's that?"

"It's a boat ride," Elvis answered, quickly.

"Oh," she said. "I think I can go on that one."

"You can." He hesitated, looked at me, and I knew what he was thinking. "Grace, you can ride with Red. He's gonna have … all the popcorn." At that, Elvis gave a nod of his head to Red, who headed over to one of the attendants to, I gathered, place a popcorn order.

"Popcorn, yay! I'm starving," she said. We all made our way to Lover's Lane. Suddenly, I wasn't so tired. My heart had picked up a few beats at the thought of a boat ride in the dark with Elvis. As long as Grace was occupied; I don't think she'd understand Elvis and me together.

The group started pairing off, as they climbed into Lover's Lane boats. Elvis held up the rear with Grace and me. True to form, Red walked up with two giant bags of popcorn. Grace ran up to him. "I'm going with you, Red, and we're gonna eat popcorn on the lover boat ride!"

He held both bags up in the air. "We're going to eat a lot of popcorn." He was a good sport, that's for sure. The operator guided Red to the next boat and lifted Grace in to join him.

She looked up at us before their boat departed. "Mama, I guess you'll ride with Elvis?"

Elvis and I looked at each other, smiled, and back at her. "I guess so," we replied in unison.

What I remember about rides like this is playing kissy face in the dark. I giggled at the memory. "What are you laughing about?" Elvis asked, and pulled me back toward him with both arms. We could hear the group poking fun at each other up ahead, even a little splashing.

"I remembered two things about this ride."

"Really," he said and started kissing the back of my neck. "And you're going to make me guess?" Chills ran up and down my spine.

"The first thing is pretty obvious."

"Mmmhmm." Now he was nibbling on my left ear. "And that is ..."

"The dark, silly. It's dark on this ride."

"Dark, yes," as he moved to kiss on my right ear, filling me with electricity.

"And the second thing is ..." I groaned softly, "happening now."

He stopped. "What's happening now?"

I turned around in the boat as best I could to face him, which ended up being sideways. "Kissing!" I whispered loudly, which brought a wolf call from up ahead.

"I don't know what you're talking about," he whispered back, and that was it. He grabbed me with both hands, tilted me backward and planted a big one right on my lips. I grabbed his face and kissed him right back.

We remained lip-locked for the rest of the ride, at least until I anticipated its end. I pulled away at that point. "Just coming up for air," I told him, and casually turned back around. I preferred that Grace not witness me kissing Elvis. It should be Chris instead, but it was so good to kiss Elvis again, after all these years.

When our boat came out of the ride, Red and Grace had just departed theirs. She was holding one of the bags of popcorn and eating out of it. My mother's instinct kicked in. "Grace, honey, I think that's enough popcorn. You don't want to get a tummy ache."

"I feel fine, Mama. And I didn't eat more than Red."

Red held up his bag of popcorn, slightly more empty than Grace's. "Guilty," he said with a smile.

Elvis climbed out of our boat and held my hand as I crossed over to the dock. "Can I have some of your popcorn, Grace?"

"Sure!" She handed her bag to him and he began to eat some as we walked away from the ride. The group was hanging out around the outside of Lover's Lane, no doubt wondering what was next.

"This is pretty good popcorn," Elvis said to the group. Red handed his bag to Sonny and they started passing it around. After a moment, Elvis said, "On second thought, it doesn't compare to the grub at Graceland. I think it's time to head out." The group seemed just fine with concluding our midnight amusement park adventure.

We walked toward the exit. Elvis pulled Red to the side to speak to him. I hoped his next wishes were to take us back to our room at the Peabody so I could get Grace to bed. I almost suggested as much, but it was as if he'd read my mind. He rejoined Grace and me and said quietly, "I think it's time to put the little one to bed."

"Yes, I agree," I replied. "Elvis, you don't have to take us to the hotel if you want to go back to Graceland, but if someone else could, that would be very helpful."

"I've got your chauffeur all lined up."

"Why, thank you!"

"Don't you wanna know who it is?" he teased.

I looked at him, remembering his lips on mine. "I have a feeling."

"Me, too," he replied with a wink.

Grace, who was trailing behind us a bit, ran up and broke our reverie. "Now I understand what being famous is!" She took Elvis' hand as we walked. "When kids find out Elvis Presley has his own theme park, you're gonna have more fans than anyone in the world!"

Elvis laughed. We all did. As we left Fairgrounds Amusement Park, I walked slightly behind Elvis and Grace so I could observe them together. She was still excited, but her energy was fading. I couldn't compute how many hours we'd been awake. She let out a big yawn. Elvis spotted it, scooped her up and carried her the rest of the way to the car.

They are my heart.

CHAPTER 20

Amazing Grace

Grace was asleep when we returned to the Peabody and I was grateful for Elvis carrying her from the car to our room because she was quite a deadweight when she was out. I unlocked the door and Elvis followed me into the room and lay Grace on the bed. She stirred when I started pulling down the covers and started to awaken when she saw Elvis. "Hey, Gracie, we're back at the hotel and it's time for bed," I said softly to her. "It's been a long day and you need some rest. Say good night to Elvis. You'll see him tomorrow."

"Good night, Elvis Presley," she said. It was cute how she called him by his first and last name. "I'm sure glad I met you and after I get a little rest, I'll be ready for another fun day tomorrow, OK?"

"Good night, Gracie," Elvis said, smiling at the old line from *Burns and Allen.* He bent down and kissed her on the forehead. "Sleep tight."

"Don't let the bed bugs bite!" Grace exclaimed and I shushed her.

Elvis rested a hand on my shoulder and whispered, "I'll be next door." He left me alone to settle Grace down, leaving through the door that connected our rooms.

I decided to slip Grace out of her jumper and into a nightgown, knowing that would relax her as well. "Will you sing me 'Amazing Grace,' Mama, please?" she asked as I helped her get changed.

"Yes, I'll sing if you quietly and calmly follow me to the bathroom to go potty and brush your teeth," I compromised.

"Yes, Mama." A few minutes later, I was tucking her back in bed with her favorite blanket and new Peabody duck. I kissed her on her dimple. "I love you, Amazing Grace."

"To infinny and beyond, Mama Llama! Now sing," she replied. I turned off the light on the nightstand so that the only remaining light was coming from the bathroom. As I brushed through her curls with my fingers to calm her, I started singing:

Amazing Grace, how sweet the sound
That saved a wretch like me
I once was lost but now am found,
Was blind but now I see

'Twas Grace that taught my heart to fear
And Grace my fears relieved
How precious did that grace appear
The hour I first believed

Through many dangers, toils and snares
I have already come
'Tis Grace has brought me safe thus far
And Grace will lead me home

By the end of the third verse, my little sweetheart was falling asleep. I sang the fourth verse just to be sure.

The Lord has promised good to me
His word my hope secures;
He will my shield and portion be,
As long as life endures

I heard a door creak. I looked over and Elvis had poked his head in. Embarrassing! I shook my head at him and gave him the "be quiet" gesture with my finger to my lips. I hummed another verse and Grace was out.

Elvis was still in the doorway. I went to him and he whispered in his baby talk, "I wanna sing 'Amazing Grace,' too, Mama!"

I smiled at him. "Next time. You'll be much better than me."

"I kinda like your voice, Moody. It could put me to sleep, too," he joked.

I gave him another "be quiet" sign and pushed him back into his room. Poking my head past the door, I added, "Hey, give me a couple of minutes and I'll be over." Not intending to, I yawned. "Sorry, it's been quite a day." Elvis grabbed me by the hand. I pulled it back. "I'll be right there."

When I crossed through the adjoining doors, Elvis was propped up in bed with the bedside radio on low. His jacket and belt were on the floor and his shirt was untucked. "Do you have to go back to Graceland tonight?" I asked.

"Nah. Red called the house and told them we were staying put because I was down with a headache." A pause. "I told Red to get his own room."

Wow. "Priscilla won't worry about you?"

Ignoring me, he beckoned, "C'mere, woman," patting the space next to him on the bed. I hesitated, and he saw it. "I'm not going to do anything you don't want me to. Now get over here and sit next to me."

I thought about being a little defiant and heading for the chair but he was impossible to resist. As I climbed onto the bed next to him, I suddenly felt shy. And guilty. "Elvis, it's been a long time. Things have changed."

"Oh, you don't say! Well, that's a mighty keen observation! Of course, they have—it's been five years!" He grabbed my leg just above the knee, which was super ticklish. I squealed and twisted away from him, then covered my mouth, remembering Grace asleep in the next room.

"Stop it!" I laughed, and playfully hit him on the chest. He made a move to grab my leg again but I grabbed his hand before he did. I took a deep breath to turn my mood back to a serious one. Looking down at his handsome hand in mine, I said what I needed to. "Elvis,

I'm not sure if I did a good thing or bad thing by coming back here. I've missed you so much." I looked him in the eye. "Every day. And I tried to come back sooner! Honest, I did. It's just … complicated."

"It sure as hell is, Maggie," Elvis said, his eyes now smoldering. I'd ruined our playful moment. "You showed up here with a kid! And I think you're trying to say she's mine!"

"Ouch, Elvis." That hurt my heart. "She's more than just a *kid*," I defended her. "She's my sweet, smart, beautiful …" My voice broke. "Amazing Grace."

"Aw, hell, I know that! She's a great kid. Don't get upset." He rolled on his side to face me. "I swear, Moody, you make me so mad, I wanna punch a wall … or kiss you!" With that, he chose the latter, grabbing my face and planting a big one on me. I about melted, again.

The two of us were riding a roller coaster of emotions: anger, confusion, hurt, frustration and passion. Still locked in a kiss, I felt every one of them and imagined he did, too. I was the first to pull away. "Elvis," I whispered.

"What?" he whispered back, in between kisses to my cheeks, nose and eyes.

"I'm glad you didn't punch a wall." That made him smile. I pulled back and our eyes met. "I'm sorry. Will you forgive me?"

He held my face in his hands. I fiddled with the collar and buttons on his shirt. "Yes. As long as you give me some time to sort this out. And don't start that time travel shit with me again." I sighed. He continued. "Let's just have a nice visit and do fun things with Grace, and my family and friends, and not think about when you need to go back home. To *Chris*."

I gave up, at least for now. His presence was so overwhelming, and he had a way of getting what he wanted. I would try to forget about all of the drama and complications, but I would not stop worrying.

Elvis' kisses had resumed and were starting to roam, along with his hands. My desire won out and I gave in to the moment.

Suddenly, Priscilla popped into my head. "Elvis," I stirred. "I want to respect your relationship with Priscilla. I know how important she is to you."

He looked up from kissing my stomach under my top. "Moody, let's make a deal. I'll handle Cilla and you handle Chris. But … we'll handle 'em later and kick 'em out of the bedroom for now. OK?"

Even though I knew it wasn't right, I close my eyes and surrendered. "OK. You're the boss." That made me grin, thinking of his *Viva Las Vegas* song with Ann-Margret.

I let him be the boss, and he made me crazy with passion. I swear he kissed me for over an hour! Everywhere. *This is the definition of foreplay, guys. Take a lesson from the King.* Elvis worked his lips from one end of my body to the other. "I want those lips on mine," I said, when he had reached my toes and was the farthest away from me than he'd been.

"Relax," he replied. "Like you said, it's been a long time, so I'm gonna take my time." And then he worked his way back up. I was coming unglued. Our lips reunited in soft, sensual kisses, smothering each other with our lust. As long as I live, his will be my favorite lips.

I couldn't take it anymore and wanted him on top of me. It was then that I realized he was still wearing clothes. He had removed mine along the way. "Hey," I teased, looking at my nakedness. "This doesn't seem fair."

"How are we going to make it fair?" he teased back.

"I'm going to take your clothes off."

"Don't mind if you do."

Finally, we were both naked, in each other's arms, and I could tell that he, too, was taken by the passion. Still in charge, Elvis climbed on top, kissing my lips, face, ears. Slowly, gently, the two of us became one. *God! I felt so lucky.* This beautiful man is loving on me and I'm giving myself to him.

It didn't take long for either of us to hit the heights—me first, followed immediately by him. I didn't want this delirious feeling to end. "Oh, Elvis," I whispered, my heart racing.

"Oh, Moody," he responded, and kissed me on the forehead. He rolled on to his back.

I nestled into the crook of his arm, his warm body against my face. I could feel his strong heartbeat on my cheek. Elvis started humming "Amazing Grace," then said, "You know, you didn't finish that song earlier."

I was so tired and contented, all that came out of me was, "Ummhmm."

Tightening his arms around me, Elvis sang the final two verses:

Yet, when this flesh and heart shall fail,
And mortal life shall cease,
I shall possess within the veil,
A life of joy and peace.

When we've been there ten thousand years
Bright shining as the sun,
We've no less days to sing God's praise
Than when we've first begun

It wasn't a lullaby, but it worked like one. The King of Rock 'n Roll sang me to sleep.

CHAPTER 21

My Little Friend

After falling asleep in the arms of Elvis, I woke up with no idea where I was. The body next to me was larger than Grace and smelled like men's cologne. My brain suddenly fired a signal that I was in bed with Elvis. *Grace!* I was instantly alert, wondering where she was. I saw light coming from a doorway and remembered that I put her to sleep in the next room.

Elvis was sound asleep. I quietly got out of bed and realized I was naked. I felt around on the floor for my clothes and crept through the adjoining door. Grace was fast asleep, too. I scurried to the bathroom and put on a robe. I closed the adjoining door and crawled into bed with Grace. My heart was pounding with the mischief of it all. Somehow, I settled down and fell back to sleep.

Grace and I woke up in the late morning and snuggled. "Mama, where's Elvis?" she asked. "I get to see him today, don't I?"

"Yes, you do," I replied, softly. "Please whisper, because he's still sleeping in the next room."

"OK," she whispered. She was quiet for a moment, then, "What are we going to do until he wakes up?"

"Well, if we can do it quietly, we can get dressed and go eat."

"I can be quiet, Mama."

We climbed out of bed and made our way to the bathroom. I grabbed our tote bag of belongings. We took a quick shower and put on our second outfits. For me, it was the two pieces from my original failed attempt to time travel four years ago: brown stretch pants with a brown and white stripe turtleneck sweater. I was happy it still fit after having a baby! For Grace, a black and white plaid jumper with yesterday's blouse. I was grateful she hadn't gotten any stains on it; it would work for a second day.

The clock on the nightstand said 10:45 a.m. "Grace, the ducks will be walking in 15 minutes. Do you want to see them again?"

"Yes!" she answered, a little too loudly. I put my index finger to my lips. "I'm taking my Peabody duck to meet the real Peabody ducks," she whispered.

We went down to the lobby and watched another identical procession of ducks. Grace was still enthralled and sat up front with the other children. I spied Red having coffee nearby. He saw me, too, and beckoned me over. I looked back at Grace and decided she would be fine for a minute or two. I headed over to Red.

"Good morning," I said.

"Morning," he replied. "As you may remember, Elvis sleeps all day." I nodded in agreement.

"I'm sure he'll want to go back to Graceland when he wakes up," he continued. Under his breath, he muttered, "Priscilla will sure as hell be wondering after him." He cleared his throat. "In the meantime, I suppose you and the little one can find something to do?"

"Sure. In fact, we need to eat something."

"Put that on Elvis' room tab," he said.

"Oh, that's not necessary, I have money." So far, the hotel had not questioned my modern-looking bills.

"Charge it," he insisted. "Elvis also cleared the way for you to go shopping at the boutique here. Just tell the sales clerks to put what you buy on his tab."

"Oh, my goodness! How generous!" I replied. "But I don't want to take advantage."

"At least get something, since he offered," he added.

"OK. Thanks, Red. I guess we'll see you later?"

"I guess." I headed back to where Grace was near the fountain.

After a nice mother-daughter brunch, we went to the boutique. I felt bad for spending Elvis' money but couldn't resist the chance to look around. I chose a navy-blue sailor dress with white piping and red scarf for Grace. For Sarah, I got a beautiful dress coat. It was baby blue and white plaid, double-breasted with big white buttons and Peter Pan collar. It fit me, too, though my sister would wear it better.

We watched a little TV in our room. I tried to keep Grace mellow, even attempted to get her to nap, but she was too excited about day two with Elvis.

Soon enough, the adjoining door open and a freshly dressed Elvis poked his head in. Ah, the sight of him! He was wearing a bright red, long-sleeve velour sweater with collar and half-zipper, with his black pants and boots. "Who wants to go to Graceland?" he asked.

Grace leapt off the bed. "I do, I do!" she exclaimed.

Elvis scooped her up into his arms, then looked at me and raised an eyebrow. I took his cue. "I do, too," I added.

"Well, then, let's get the show on the road!" he said, and gave me a wink.

Red was waiting in the hallway. He led us to a service elevator, which took me a second to figure out why: Elvis would cause a scene if we left through the main lobby. On the ground level, we followed Red to a back entrance, where Elvis' black Cadillac was waiting for him. Elvis motioned for me to get in the front seat. Grace got in the back seat with Red.

"Yay! We're going to your house!" she proclaimed, bouncing in the back seat. "Graceland is a house with my name in it." I almost told her to fasten her seatbelt but caught myself; it wasn't really a practice in the '60s.

Elvis laughed and looked at Grace in the rearview mirror. "Good point, Gracie. Do you know how Graceland got its name?"

She pondered that for a second. "Well, I'm only 4 so I don't think it could be from me."

Elvis laughed again. "Not that I don't think a house should be named for you, but my house goes back to when it was built in the 1930s and the first owners named it for their Aunt Grace."

"Aunt Grace," she repeated. "Maybe if I grow up to be an aunt someday, I'll get a house named after me, too!" Grace was quiet only a few seconds. "Elvis, do we get to go on a tour of Graceland? Mama said she'd take me on a tour of Graceland."

Time to cover. I saw the strange look on Elvis' face. "Grace, honey, I know you're excited, but try to calm down a little." My eyes dashed over for a quick glance at Red, who made immediate eye contact with me. "Sit back and sit still for a few minutes while we drive."

"I'll show you all around the house, Grace," Elvis said. "And the front yard and the back yard, the whole place. I'll even introduce you to someone very special."

Grace could hardly contain her excitement, but she was a good girl and her next question was more tempered. "Who, Elvis, who?"

"A beautiful little baby doll like you," he answered. "My Priscilla." Elvis reached for my hand at gave it a squeeze.

Priscilla. Oh, my! Here we go.

When Elvis pulled up to the gates of Graceland, even I had to contain my excitement. It was so good to be back—and with him, no less. I kept my cool, however, hoping to keep Grace calm. Quite honestly, I was nervous about meeting the love of Elvis' life. What was Priscilla going to think about me? And how was he going to treat me around her?

"Hey, Uncle," Elvis said out the rolled-down window and came to a stop.

"Hello, son," Uncle Travis replied while peering into the car at the rest of us. I thought to myself that there could be no way he would recognize me, given how many people have come and gone through these gates.

Red, who'd been quiet on the drive here, grabbed his door handle. "Hey, boss," he said to Elvis. "I'll get out here. I need to talk to

Travis about a couple of things." He was looking at me when he said that.

"I bet you have security guard stuff to take care of, don't you, Red?" Grace inquired.

That brought a smile. "Right, Miss Grace, I sure do. I'll see you a little later, up at the house."

"Okie dokie!" She turned her attention to me, leaning forward into the front seat. "Mama, I'm so happy to be at Graceland!"

"I know, baby." I patted her little hands. "I am, too."

Elvis drove us up the driveway and around to the carport to park the car. We got out of the car and he opened the back door to let Grace scramble out.

Grace was wide-eyed, looking around at the mansion and the big back yard. Elvis stepped beside her and put his hand on her shoulder. "Welcome to Graceland, Gracie. Welcome to my home."

She turned to look up at him and reached for his hand. Elvis scooped her up into his arms. That made my heart flutter. He headed to the back door with her. I followed.

Over his shoulder, Grace looked back at me. "Mama, it looks just like the pictures." I cringed. I needed time to figure out an explanation, especially since Elvis hadn't taken me seriously any of the times I tried to tell him the truth.

"Pictures, huh?" Elvis said to Grace, turning back toward me. "Well, I don't know about that, but now you get to see the real thing." He tickled her stomach and she giggled. "Let's go inside first and see what's cookin'."

The wonderful aromas from the kitchen hit us before we got there. It smelled like hot biscuits—right out of the oven—and hot dogs. My stomach growled. Alberta was at her station.

"VO5!" Elvis exclaimed. "I've brought some friends with me and if they're as hungry as I am, it's time for you to work your magic. What do we got to eat?"

"Well, I declare!" Alberta answered. "Who in the world is this pretty little missus?" Then she answered Elvis' question. "Mr. Elvis, we've got wieners and biscuits, just like you like 'em, with sauerkraut."

Grace was still in Elvis' arms, her eyes wide open, taking it all in. I stood beside him near the counter. Elvis jostled her in his arms. "This is Grace," he said. "And this is her mama Maggie … a friend of mine … from way back. They're visiting Memphis." As he said this, he was looking at me and gave another wink. I suppose he wanted me to go along with his story, whatever that would turn out to be.

"Miss Grace, I've seen a lot of pretty girls come and go, but you may be the prettiest!" Alberta said. "Are you hungry, child? And how about you, Miss Maggie?" She paused as her memory undoubtedly jogged. "You know, you look familiar. Have I seen you before?"

I wasn't sure how to reply so I glanced first at Elvis. He nodded slightly. "Why, yes, Alberta. It's been a few years, but I visited here before, for a few days. I remember you, too."

"Well, it's mighty nice to see you again, Miss Maggie. You hungry, too?"

I laughed, perhaps from my nerves. "A little bit, yes."

"Well, then, let's get to work filling some tummies." Elvis ordered for the three of us. We would be having hot dogs and biscuits. That sounded wonderful to me and they were foods that Grace liked, too, minus the sauerkraut.

Elvis sat Grace on the edge of the counter and she became preoccupied with watching Alberta prepare our plates. "Where's Priscilla?" he asked, heading to the back staircase. "Cilla! I'm home! Where are you, girl? Come on down. I've got some friends here I want you to meet."

I held my breath. Was I really about to meet the future Mrs. Presley? No sooner did I have that thought, I heard the sound of footsteps coming down the back stairs. And there she was: Priscilla Beaulieu. A stunning, petite beauty, looking a bit unhappy. Her hair was just like in photos: straight and smooth in front, teased into a big beehive in back, with sections curled and left hanging down.

"Hey, baby," Elvis said softly, moving to her and wrapping her in a big hug, with kisses to her lips, cheek and ear. "How's my Little One? I missed you. Did you miss me?"

She looked up at him, unaffected by his baby talk. "You didn't come home last night," she said, softly.

"Oh, Satnin, I had such a bad headache, I stayed at the hotel, baby. I couldn't even open my eyes." He caressed her dark hair and kissed her on the forehead. "I love you, Little One." Her expression began to warm. There he goes, getting away with murder.

With his arm around her, Elvis escorted Priscilla into the kitchen. She was truly beautiful, a perfect little doll. She was wearing a bright red collared top with long, puffy sleeves and a little white accent bow at the V-neck. Tight white stretch pants and brown penny loafers completed her look. Her entrance cast a spell upon Grace. Elvis pinched Grace's cheek. "Cilla, this is Grace." He motioned to me. "And my old friend Maggie."

Old. Ha. I quickly did the math; Priscilla was 20 and I was 14 years older. "Girls, this is my baby, Priscilla," Elvis continued with the introductions.

Her shyness was easy to see, in the way she batted her eyes and made little eye contact. "Nice to meet you," she replied softly. She stayed close to Elvis. I was in a bit of a trance, and conflicted. Part of me was enthralled to meet her. The other part, if I'm being honest, wished she wasn't in the picture.

Alberta served our meal, which smelled heavenly. Hot dogs slathered with sauerkraut, and hot biscuits on the side. We sat at the counter. Elvis perched Grace on his lap and put her plate in between us. We dove into our meals. Priscilla sipped on an iced tea. As it goes when folks are eating, the atmosphere was quiet.

Grace finished first and it didn't take long for her to start fidgeting. "Mama, I want to see the other rooms."

I reached for her and pulled her from Elvis' lap so he could finish his meal. "I know you do, Grace. Can you give us a few more minutes to finish eating? And how about you take a few more bites?"

She took another bite of hot dog, then turned her attention to Priscilla on the other side of Elvis. I'd seen that look before, when she watched her Disney movies. She thought she was looking at a princess.

Priscilla noticed the little girl gazing at her. "Grace, if you'd like, I'll take you on a tour of the house."

"You will?" she said, turning to me. "Mama, is it OK?"

"Of course, it is," Elvis answered for me. I nodded at them, too. "Show her around the first floor, Cilla, while we finish up here. I want to take Gracie down to the basement. That's where the fun is."

Grace jumped off my lap. Priscilla held out her hand and Grace put her little hand inside. As they headed toward the front of the house, Grace turned to me with a precious look on her face; she was enamored.

Alone in the kitchen, except for Alberta, Elvis and I finished eating. And, boy, could Elvis eat. I think he devoured four hot dogs!

Unbeknownst to Alberta, he put his hand on my leg behind the counter. That startled me a bit. Our eyes met. He whispered, "I appreciate you rolling with it. I want to spend time with you, but this is the way things are at Graceland. I want to spend more time *alone* with you, too, so we'll figure it out." In a voice loud enough for Albert to hear, Elvis continued, "What do you say, Maggie, shall we join the tour group?" Patting his full stomach, he added, "Thank you, VO5, you've done it again." We both got up and headed out of the kitchen.

Wow. When you're the King of Rock 'n Roll, I guess you get what you want, whenever you want it.

Elvis took me by the hand and led me out of the kitchen, toward the front of the house. "Cilla! Where are ya?" he yelled down the hallway. I looked around, giddy to be back at Graceland.

Elvis smartly let go of my hand when we heard the sounds of piano keys being plucked. I hoped Grace was behaving herself. We headed through the parlor into the music room, where Elvis had a beautiful white baby grand piano that he'd bought from Memphis' Ellis Auditorium. Sure enough, Grace was at the bench with Priscilla standing nearby. She gave me a strange look. Protective of her man, she joined his side.

"Mama, I met Elvis' grandma, Minnie Mae!" Grace exclaimed, over the cacophony of piano keys.

"Did you? Great!" I replied.

"She was in her room. And now I'm playing Elvis Presley's piano!"

"Is that what it's called?" Elvis teased, and looked at me. "Maybe your Mama should get you some lessons."

"Well, I'm not very good because I don't know any songs yet!" That made Elvis laugh and he joined her on the bench.

"I do. What do you say I play one for you?" He began to play "Wooden Heart," which Grace knew. We'd watched *GI Blues* many times.

When Elvis finished playing and singing, Grace looked at him pensively and said, "I think it would hurt to have a wooden heart. What if you got a splinter?" She put her little hands over her heart. "Ouch!"

Elvis cracked up and scooted off the bench toward Priscilla, wrapping his arms around her and kissing her on the forehead. "No wooden hearts here. No splinters, no ouchies." I looked away. Elvis changed the mood. "Let's go down to the basement and have some fun!" He and Priscilla headed out of the music room.

"Yay!" Grace replied and scurried off the bench, happily following them. I brought up the rear. *A little ouch,* I thought.

This was definitely the most interesting basement Grace has ever seen. Elvis took us first to the entertainment room. He plopped down on one of the couches and Priscilla sat beside him. I remained back a bit and leaned against the bar. Grace stood in the center of the room, taking in the comfy furnishings and three identical TVs set in the wall, inspired by President Johnson's Oval Office. She noticed the jukebox and approached it slowly. "What's this?"

"That's a jukebox, Gracie," he answered. "It plays music. Let me show you how to play a song." He got up and met her at the music machine.

"What songs does it play? I bet it plays Elvis Presley!" Grace giggled, looking up at him. I almost jumped in to tell her Elvis actually didn't like to listen to himself sing, but he beat me to it.

"If I'm going to sing, it's gonna be live and in person." He punched some of the buttons. "Let's find something else you'd like to hear." Sam the Sham and the Pharaohs started singing "Wooly Bully."

Grace started grooving to the music. She was a free spirit when it came to dancing, just like her mother. Her moves made me smile. Priscilla, too.

Elvis laughed again. He danced with Grace a bit before sitting back down. Realizing all eyes were on her, she had a moment of shyness, and ran and jumped into a big chair.

"Hey, what about the dance show? I wanna see more!" Elvis said. To that, Grace wiggled around in her chair. When that brought more laughter, she stood up in her chair to dance.

"Now, now, Grace, sit back down," I admonished her. "You know we don't stand on the furniture."

"It's OK, Maggie," Elvis said. "This is one lived in room. Why don't you stop being a wall flower and join us?" He winked at me.

Grace wasn't sure if she should listen to me or Elvis. She wisely hopped out of her chair and danced some more. The jukebox paused for a moment to change songs, then The Searchers' "Love Potion #9" played.

"Dance with me, Mama!" Grace said, reaching for me. *Great*. I get to dance in front of Elvis and Priscilla. I decided to make the most of it. My girl and I boogied to the beat. Elvis got a kick out of it and bounced his legs and clapped along. I noticed even Priscilla seemed to be enthused.

When the song ended, Grace was ready to move on. "What's in that room?" she asked as she tiptoed toward the next room.

This time, I followed her first. "That's the pool room, Grace." Anticipating her next words, I continued. "Not a swimming pool. Elvis has one of those outside. But pool as in billiards. You know this game, right?" I pointed to the big green pool table in the center of the room. Red and Sonny were in the middle of a game so I held her back, out of the way of their cues.

"Oh, yeah, Poppy helped me play this at Gigi's house. He had to give me a boost because I'm too little." Elvis and Priscilla, moving again as a single unit, entered the room.

"Hi, Sonny. Hi, Red," I said. "Grace, do you remember Sonny from last night?"

"Hello there, cutie pie!" Sonny responded.

"Is your name sunny because you're like sunshine?" Grace asked.

Sonny laughed. "Actually, it's a nickname, which is a good thing because my real name is Delbert. Delbert B. West. But you can call me Sonny. S-o-n-n-y."

"Sonny West and Red West are cousins," I said.

Grace skipped over to the cousin she knew best. "Are you winning, Red?"

"It's Sonny's turn now, but I think I'll be winning after that," Red answered.

We watched them play for a bit. Sonny accidentally sunk the cue ball on a move. "I think the white ball is supposed to stay on the table, right Grace?" Elvis joked. The mood was light, but I knew these guys were competitive with each other so I suggested we continue our tour so they could finish their game. "Let's go to the den," Elvis said, and led the way.

"Bye, bye, cousins!" Grace yelled behind her as we exited. We heard Sonny say, "See you later, alligator!" as we headed upstairs.

When we entered the den, I realized I may be the only person who knew this space would one day become the Jungle Room.

It was far from that now. Thick curtains darkened the space. The furniture wasn't the outlandish, oversized dark wood pieces Elvis would one day buy as a joke on his father. This den contained several round tables, two big leather couches and a large leather chair fit for a king. It faced a big TV—very big for 1965.

Grace jumped into Elvis' big chair. "Let's watch a movie!"

"Maybe later, Grace," I said. "We're still have to see the outside."

Grace hopped out of the chair and took my hand. "Elvis, I like your man cave."

"Man cave, ha!" Elvis said with a laugh. "I like that." I cringed. Another modern idiom tossed backward in time.

We headed outside and to the swimming pool. Too bad it was out of season. Grace would have loved to swim at Graceland. The pool was a sparkling blue, inviting and deceiving on a sunny October day. "Mama, can we go swimming?" Grace asked.

"I'm afraid the water's a little too cold right now," Elvis answered. He squatted down to stick his hand in the water. "Come here and see."

She joined him, putting her little hand in for a dip. "Oooh, yeah, it's chilly willy!" She shook her hand, splashing some drops on Elvis.

"Hey, no fair!" Elvis said and flicked a few drops her way.

Grace shrieked, and reached into the pool again to splash Elvis. I raced to her. "Grace, let's not start a water fight, please. Elvis just said the water's too cold."

"It's OK," Elvis said. "It's gotta be hard for any kid to be near a pool and not want to splash. It's hard for me," he added.

While we were on the pool patio, I noticed someone leaving Vernon's office out of the corner of my eye. It was Patsy! "Elvis," I said quickly. "Can you watch Grace for a minute? I want to run over and say hello to Patsy."

"Yes, ma'am, we will," he replied. He was still attached at the hip to Priscilla.

I made my way toward the office. "Patsy! It's so good to see you again!" I ran to embrace her in a big hug, then hesitated. "Wait, do you remember me? Maggie, from a few years ago?"

A second later, Patsy broke into a smile. "Of course, I remember you, Maggie. Come here," she said, shifting the batch of mail she was carrying, and opened her arms for the hug. We embraced and she spoke quietly. "A lot of girls come and go from Graceland, but you're one of the memorable ones." Her facial expression changed to a serious one. "You disappeared without a trace." She cocked her head and looked at me inquisitively. "Why did you leave like that?" She lowered her voice to a whisper. "You know, he was quite upset." As she said that, she nodded her head toward Elvis, who was still in the pool area.

"I know that now, and I can explain. Let's make some introductions, then see if we can sneak away for a little girl talk," I replied. "I've thought about you many times and know I owe you an explanation." I grabbed her hand in mine. "You deserve to understand what happened then, and what's happened since."

Patsy patted my hand. "OK, Maggie. I'll be curious to hear your story." Louder, her next words were meant for us to rejoin the group. "Hey ya'll! Who do we have there, a pretty little girl who's come to visit Graceland?"

Grace, who'd been standing by Elvis, bounded over to Patsy and me. "Grace, I want to introduce you to someone." She walked closer to us. "This is Patsy Presley—Elvis' double first cousin."

Grace took my hand and asked, "What's a double first cousin?"

I laughed, stroked her curls and continued the introductions before answering her question. "Patsy, this is my daughter, Grace."

"My goodness!" Patsy exclaimed. "What a darling girl you are. Nice to meet you, Grace." She leaned in and extended a hand to Grace. They shook hands "A lovely name, too," Patsy continued. "Welcome, Grace, to Graceland!"

"Thank you," Grace replied. I was thankful my little one remembered her manners. Grace jumped back to her question. "What's a double first cousin?" She looked at me. "Do I have one, Mama?"

As Patsy elaborated, Elvis and Priscilla headed our way. "Well, Elvis' daddy, Vernon, and my daddy, Vester, are brothers. That makes us cousins. What makes us *double* cousins is that Elvis' mama, Gladys and my mama, Clettes, were sisters. Two brothers married two sisters, making their kids double first cousins."

Grace shook her head. "There's so many cousins here!" she said, and everyone laughed.

"Yep, we're a big, goofy family," Elvis said.

"Oh!" I jumped in. "I just remembered. I have something for you, Patsy. Let me run inside and get it from my bag." I headed to the house. I noticed the group heading back to sit on the patio.

Patsy had turned her attention to Grace. "So, Miss Grace, what do you think of Graceland?"

"Well, I thought it would be bigger, but it's just the right size for a kid like me," she answered. The adults laughed.

"Bigger! My goodness," Patsy said. "Graceland seems plenty big to me."

"Well, Cinderella lives in a really big castle," Grace countered. "I haven't seen it in person yet, but Mama's gonna take me there some day."

I returned just in the nick of time, catching Grace's last comment. She was referring to Disney World, a Florida theme park that was six years away from opening.

"I ain't no Cinderella," Elvis said. "So I don't live in a castle."

Grace giggled. "No, you're Elvis Presley! Graceland is your castle." Looking at Priscilla, she got googly eyed again. "And Priscilla is your princess."

"Yes, she is, my beautiful little princess," Elvis baby talked and squeezed Priscilla even closer to him.

Gift in hand, I welcomed the distraction. "Patsy, this is for you." I handed her a scarf that was unique for this time period.

Patsy wasn't sure what I'd given her. "It's an infinny scarf!" Grace informed her. "Like Buzz Lightyear infinny and beyond."

"Grace," I interrupted. She'd just given a *Toy Story* movie reference.

"Infinny and beyond?" Patsy asked. "I think I'm going to need a little help with that."

"Infinity," I said. "You see, it's a big loop scarf." I unfolded the scarf to its original shape. I'd chosen a simple pattern of small pastel flowers.

"I think it might be too big for me?" Patsy inquired.

"It's called an infinity scarf because there are several ways to wear it." As I said this, Grace took the scarf from me and walked to Patsy, who was seated, and reached up to put it over Patsy's head. Then, like a little fashionista, she crisscrossed the loop and put the bottom portion over Patsy's head, too. She adjusted and fluffed the scarf until it looked good on all sides.

"There," Grace said, satisfied with her attempt. "This is a way to wear infinny scarves." I glanced at Priscilla; Grace had her complete attention and I silently wished I'd brought more than one of these with me.

Patsy looked down at Grace's handiwork. "I think I need to see this in a mirror." Looking at me, she added, "Thanks, Maggie, for my *infinny* scarf."

Elvis had stepped away to Vernon's office while we were with Patsy. "Gracie, come here," he beckoned out the door. "I want you to meet my Daddy."

"Your Daddy?" She took off running. Priscilla followed.

"I'm going to try putting Grace down for a nap," I said to Patsy. "If you've got some time in a little while, maybe we could chat?"

"Sounds good," she replied.

I headed to Vernon's office, the place where he managed Elvis' finances, fan mail and personal business. He was tight with a dollar, having grown up poor. I imagined how he reacted to Elvis' extravagant purchases.

Truthfully, the space didn't look much different than it does on the Graceland tour. Bulky, metal desks and tall file cabinets. Plain curtains and carpet. A comfy looking leather couch. Several mailbags full of fan mail was a different sight. Had Elvis been alive today, he'd be getting tweets instead.

Vernon, usually a serious guy, was smiling as he interacted with Grace. He was behind his desk and she was sitting on Elvis' lap on the couch.

"Daddy, this is Maggie, Grace's Mama," Elvis said, acknowledging me as I entered the room. Priscilla had gone to sit beside her man. Vernon nodded at me. "They're visiting Memphis from St. Louis, and they're going to stay at Graceland tonight," he added, looking at me.

"We are?" Grace shrieked, happily. "A sleepover at Graceland!" She was thrilled and bounced on his lap. Priscilla looked less delighted.

"I don't see why not, Miss Grace," Vernon said. "Graceland is one big sleepover. That is, when people actually sleep."

"Nice to see you, Vernon," I said to him, then turned my attention to Elvis and Grace. "We'll see how the day goes, Grace," I said. "It's a very kind invitation from Elvis and *maybe* we can spend the night, if you take a nap."

"I'll take a nap, Mama, I promise," Grace said, emphatically. Elvis dipped her in his arms and started rocking and singing a lullaby. That only prompted giggles from her and tickling from him. The two of them plucked at my heart strings.

Despite their silliness, the room had an air of awkwardness to it. I thought it might be time to let Vernon get back to his work. "Grace, why don't you come with me to the Meditation Garden to settle down a bit," I said to her. Dutifully, she climbed down from Elvis' lap and came over to take my hand. Looking at Elvis and Priscilla, I added, "We'll give you two a break."

Elvis faked a yawn and stretch, and put his arm around his beauty. "OK. What do you say, Little One? Wanna head back to the house?"

Priscilla looked at him with doe eyes full of admiration. "Yes, my love."

With that, we all left the office, going our separate ways.

Grace and I walked the short distance to the Meditation Garden, which was, at this time, quite new. Elvis had it built in 1964 and '65 as a place for contemplation. The King wanted a private retreat, to think about his problems and other things on his mind. Grace was immediately taken with the centerpiece, a circular pool with fountain jets. "Mama, a fountain! Can we throw in a penny and make a wish?"

I didn't see any pennies in the water. "Not now, Grace. You know what we're going to do? We're going to sit on this bench and think of something to wish for, something to pray for, because that's what this garden is all about. Thinking, praying and wishing." I led her over to the bench and she climbed into my lap, facing me for some hug time. "It's been a pretty busy day so far and we've seen a lot of new things." I started rocking her, hoping for the best. "Let's think about what we're grateful for. You go first."

"I'm grateful for Elvis!" she exclaimed, shooting her head back from where it had been on my chest.

"Ssshhh," I said and put her head back on my chest. "Let's make a quiet list." In a softer voice, I continued. "I'm grateful for Elvis, too. May God bless him and watch over him."

"And Priscilla. God bless Priscilla, the princess of Graceland," she said quietly.

"Yes." Things were, I guessed, as they should be.

"And Alberta."

"Yes."

"And Patsy."

"Yes."

"And Elvis' Daddy." A pause. "I forgot his name."

"Vernon. Yes. God bless Vernon and all of Elvis' family and friends."

I thought Grace was drifting off, but after a moment, she said, "I'm grateful for Graceland."

"Me, too. God bless Graceland."

While I rocked my little girl to sleep in Elvis' Meditation Garden,

I admired its architecture once again—the semi-circular pergola and white columns, the brick wall with its stained glass panels. It really was a place of peace and calm. I took a deep breath and exhaled slowly when I realized what was missing from this garden—four graves.

I closed my eyes and said a prayer.

CHAPTER 22

Spinout

I was startled by a soft touch on my shoulder. Grace was pressed against me, passed out. Priscilla crept quietly from behind me. Whispering, she said, "Let's go lay her down inside."

As gently as I could with Grace's dead weight on top of me, I got up and followed Priscilla from the Meditation Garden to the house. She led me to the front room, and the long white couch in the parlor. I laid Grace down and Priscilla found a blanket to cover her. "She may roll off in her sleep," I whispered, "so I think I'll stay nearby." I was considering curling up with Grace and taking a nap.

"OK," Priscilla said. "I think the guys are gearing up to ride go karts. I'm not sure how much longer it will be quiet." She headed outside.

She was right. Before long, I heard the distant sound of engines revving. *This should be entertaining*. The roaring grew louder as the go karts made their way to the front of the property. Grace was still sound asleep. I carried one of the dining room chairs across the entryway and put it up against the couch, in case she rolled over in her sleep. Curiosity getting the better of me, I headed out the front door to see what the guys were up to.

What a bunch of goofballs. They mostly chased Elvis; he was nearly always in the lead. They raced up and down the big, long Graceland driveway. It was so loud!

Patsy must have been attracted by the noise, too. I didn't hear her approach. "Hey there!" I yelled over the engines.

"Hi, Maggie," she said loudly. "I had to come out and see what was going on." She was still wearing her new infinity scarf.

I motioned back to the house. “Grace is taking a nap in the parlor. Do you want to have our talk before she wakes up?”

“Sure,” she replied. “Let’s try to chat here. We could go inside, but Elvis likes the attention.”

As soon as she said that, Elvis flew by on a go kart, dressed all in black, and waved at us. We waved back.

We sat on the front steps. The noise was actually a nice cover for our conversation. I wasn’t exactly willing to share my true story with everyone. There were a few girls hanging around, but they were more interested in Elvis and the boys. Priscilla and Joan, Joe’s wife, were at the supposed start-finish line, waving race flags.

“First, Patsy, I want to apologize for leaving without saying goodbye,” I began another explanation. “I’m sorry. I didn’t mean to upset anyone.” I looked for some acceptance in her eyes.

“Well, you made Elvis mad, that’s for sure. He’s got that fiery temper and your disappearance really ate at him for a while. But you know Elvis—he doesn’t spend much time alone and there’s always a pretty girl to catch his eye.”

No doubt. “You were really kind to me, Patsy. I felt like an outsider when I first arrived at Graceland. When I tell you where I came from, you’ll know what I mean.” She was about to say something but I continued. “You went out of your way to make me feel better and I’m grateful. You could have just sent me down the driveway, but you helped me get my head on straight and made it possible for me to meet Elvis Presley.”

“That I did.” She nodded. “What do you mean, where you came from> You’re from St. Louis, right?” she asked.

“Yes, but there’s a little more to it than that.”

“Oh, really?”

I took a deep breath. “The day we met, I had woken up in your storage room in the basement.” Again, Patsy started to comment, but I kept going. “I was confused and scared, especially when I figured out it was December 1960. In fact, you rescued me from freaking out about that.” A pause. “The reason I was upset was …

I came from another place. Another place, and another time. I came from the year 2006, Patsy. From the future."

Our eyes were locked. For the moment, she was emotionless. I had no idea what her reaction was going to be until she started laughing. *Here we go again*. Why does everyone laugh when I tell them this?

"Oh, Maggie, that's a good one," she said, giggling. "A real good one."

We noticed Richard nearby, getting out of his go kart. As he headed up the driveway in our direction, I said, "Patsy, I'm serious. If you don't believe me, I'll show you proof."

"Proof? Of the future?" She laughed. "It's time to get your head on straight again, young lady, or Elvis will tear into you."

"What's so funny?" Richard asked us. "Are you laughing at me, running out of gas?"

"No," Patsy replied. "Maggie here's just telling me a funny story."

Richard headed around back, presumably to fetch a gas can.

I decided to switch gears. "Let's back up for a minute to the reason why I left. I was getting homesick. I had a great time with Elvis and everyone, but when I woke up that morning, I knew I had to go back."

"To St. Louis."

"Yes, to St. Louis. And to December 2006." She laughed again. "I know it sounds nutty, and you can go on laughing, but listen to me, too, because I'm going to tell you why it's taken five years for me to come back." Patsy tried to stifle her giggling. "I returned to where I came from, to my life, through some sort of time travel." I decided not to elaborate about Chris. "It wasn't very long before I realized I was pregnant." No more laughter. "Yes, I'm talking about Grace. She came along and changed my life. I never stopped trying to get back to Elvis, though. I tried several times. Nothing worked until this time, when I brought Grace with me."

Patsy's wheels were turning. "Why did you bring Grace with you, Maggie?" Her eyes narrowed. "What are you up to?"

"I'm not 'up to' anything. I brought Grace with me because I wanted her to know Elvis. And I wanted him to know her. He could be her father." There. I said it.

She looked stunned. "Oh, he is not gonna like this."

Richard walked past us again, this time with a gas can. I was glad for the noise of the other go karts.

"Elvis is still processing," I continued, trying to sound confident. "I'm not exactly sure how he feels."

"You told him? What did he say?"

"He just laughed at me, like you did, and told me I was crazy."

"Maggie, I'm sorry, but you have to know how all of this sounds. Elvis is rich and famous. You're not the first girl who's tried to pin fatherhood on him."

She was right, and these people were probably never going to believe my story. "I didn't come here to convince anyone of anything, or 'pin' anything on anyone. I came so that Elvis and Grace could know each other." I touched her arm. "When it comes to you, Patsy, I just want to say I'm sorry that I left the way I did, and thanks for all you did for me. I really appreciated your friendship then. I hope we can still be friends."

"Apology accepted." She paused. "There's something different about you, Maggie. But you better be darn careful around Elvis. I mean it! He won't put up with any bull. He'll toss you and your little one right out of here." She made eye contact with her next words. "And don't you hurt him. He doesn't deserve that."

"I don't want to hurt anyone. I *won't* hurt anyone," I promised. We were quiet for a few seconds. "Friends?" I asked.

"Friends," she nodded in return.

"Oh, thank goodness!" I hugged her, then adjusted her scarf. "This looks really good on you. Remember the one you let me wear?"

"No, I don't!" We both laughed.

The front door opened and Mary—one of the maids—poked her head out. "Miss Maggie, there's a sad little girl inside callin' for her

Mama, and someone named Poppy."

I jumped up. I could hear Grace crying inside. "She's just a little upset," Mary reassured me. I hurried past her to the parlor.

"Mama, Mama!" Grace cried. "I woke up and couldn't remember where I was and it scared me. I want Poppy!"

I sat on the couch, picked her up and put her on my lap. "It's alright, Grace, you're at Graceland and I'm right here." I kissed her and smoothed her curls. "You fell asleep, remember? We were in the Meditation Garden."

"Yes," she whined. "But why did you put me on this couch with a chair by my head?"

"I moved you inside and laid you down so you could be more comfortable." I rocked her some. "When I needed to step away, I put the chair here so you wouldn't roll off the couch."

She gave me a serious look. "Mama, I don't like that chair. I'm a big girl now! I won't fall out of bed." She whimpered again. "I miss Poppy."

"It's alright, Grace," I soothed her. "I know you do. I miss him, too." I wondered if it was time to go home.

In the distance, engines came and went. Shrugging off the rest of her sleep, Grace sat up. "What's that noise outside, Mama?"

"Go karts. Elvis and his buddies are racing around the driveway. Wanna go take a look?"

"Yes, yes!" She scrambled off my lap, her blues forgotten.

When we returned to the front porch, Patsy had gone. "Where's Elvis?" Grace asked, searching for him.

"He'll come by soon, honey. Let's get ready to wave to him."

We waited a minute or so. A few of the golf carts whizzed by, carrying with them shouts of friendly competition mixed with laughter. It looked like fun. When Elvis raced by, he saw Grace and yelled out, "Hey Grace! I'll be back to pick you up later!"

She squealed and clapped her hands. "I get to go for a ride, Mama?"

"We'll see, Grace. I want to talk to Elvis first. I don't want him driving that fast with you."

"Don't worry, Mama! Elvis will take care of me." While I didn't doubt that he would, he did seem like a daredevil babysitter.

In between cars flying by the front of the house, Grace noticed the giant lion statues that flanked the front entrance. We visited both marble beauties. With my assistance, Grace petted their manes. I knew that Elvis had seen them in someone else's yard, when he didn't have any money. Later, when he did, he offered the owners $1,000 and had them moved to Graceland.

"Do the lions have names, Mama?" Grace asked.

"I'm not sure. We'll have to ask Elvis."

"If they don't, maybe I could name them."

I smiled. "Maybe. Got any ideas?"

"Well, I was thinking Simba and Nala, but they're both boys. So Simba could work for one. Maybe Nimba for the other because they look like twins! Simba and Nimba." She paused, her little wheels spinning. "Do you think Elvis has seen *The Lion King*?"

"No, I don't." Not possible. "Let's give the lions a rest and watch some more go kart races."

"OK. Bye, Simba. Bye, Nimba."

Elvis eventually grew tired of racing. More go karts ran out of gas. He was true to his word, and stopped by the front of the house. With my permission and his promise to drive safely, he strapped Grace in with him and went for a slower ride around the property. I remained on the front steps to wave as they passed by. Each time they did, my heart warmed at the sight of the two of them together.

CHAPTER 23

It Keeps Right On A-Hurtin'

"What are we doing tonight, boss?" Joe asked. We were lounging around the basement.

"Let's order a movie," Elvis replied. "Bring some adventure to the basement." He looked relaxed in baby blue pants, white button-down shirt and orange velour V-neck sweater. "Why don't you see if you can get the reels for *Von Ryan's Express*. We'll spend a couple hours with Sinatra."

"I'm on it."

Ordering a movie was certainly outlandish for 1965, probably something only Elvis could do. A fair amount of preparation activity began. Priscilla and some of the girls went up to make popcorn in the kitchen. A Frank Sinatra train movie sounded fun, but it had been a long day and I was thinking Grace and I needed some rest. I decided to chime in. "It's getting late. Grace and I probably need to go back to the hotel so I can put her to bed."

"No, Mama!" Grace whined. "I'm not tired."

"You're staying here," Elvis said. "It'll be easier. We can have some more fun tomorrow. If it's a nice day, we'll take the motorcycles out. I gotta break in my new Harley."

"Yay!" Grace squealed. She was not getting on a motorcycle with anyone.

"That's kind of you, Elvis, but I don't want to intrude."

"You're not. Moon can give up his apartment in the annex for the night." I figured Moon was Elvis' nickname for Marty when I saw the surprised look on Marty's face.

"Oh. OK." I paused. "I'm sorry to ask, but would it be possible to make a quick trip to the Peabody to get a few of our things?"

"Sure." Elvis replied. "Red can run you downtown and back." Looking at Red, he added, "Try not to make her cry again." He was referring to yesterday at the Peabody.

"I won't boss," Red replied, a bit sullen. Elvis had one more request, which he gave quietly to Red while his eyes were on me.

I guess it was serendipitous to have the car ride with Red. I needed to follow up on our previous conversation when I promised I'd show him proof of the future, and of Elvis' demise. It was not going to be easy to drop this subject matter on one of Elvis' best friends.

I asked Patsy to keep an eye on Grace so she didn't have to tag along with us to the Peabody. I grabbed my purse that contained the envelope I'd prepared for this moment.

The ride with Red began in silence. I knew he wasn't crazy about me, but at least he'd warmed up to Grace.

"Red," I began, staring straight ahead. "At the Peabody yesterday, when we spoke about where I came from, and I told you about Elvis, I promised you proof." I ran my hand down the length of the envelope on my lap. "I have something to tell you, Red, and show you. I think this is a good time to do that."

He looked my way. "Why is now a good time? I'm driving."

"Elvis is back at the house, otherwise occupied. You know how he gets. He wagged his finger at us yesterday and just now told you not to make me cry again."

"I supposed you're right," he agreed. "I'm just not sure I'm in the mood for what you're about to tell me. I mean, you already told me he's going to die, for Christ's sake."

I shifted in my seat so I could face him. "Red, I'm really sorry. This is a complicated situation. I've thought it over and decided that someone—meaning you—needs to know about Elvis. It's your job to take care of him, so maybe, just maybe, you can make a difference for his future."

"Maggie, you know as well as I do that no one tells Elvis Presley what to do," Red countered.

"You're right. I can't argue with that. But as his protector, I need to show you this." I slowly removed the contents of the envelope onto my lap. Red looked over at the pieces of paper.

I steeled myself for the comments I prepared. "Those pills that Elvis takes are going to be his downfall." Pause. "They're going to cause health problems." Longer pause. "They're going to contribute to his death at age of 42." I looked away, out my window. Thinking about Elvis' death always hurt me. "On August 16, 1977, Elvis is going to die of a heart attack, right here at Graceland, upstairs in his bathroom."

Red hit the steering wheel with his hand. "Maggie, how can you sit here so calmly and say things like that?!" He shook his head repeatedly.

"This is how, Red, this is how." I pointed to the copies of news clippings I'd gathered from the time of Elvis' death and funeral, knowing full well Red could choose to believe they were fakes. "You can pull over to the side of the road, or we can wait until we get to the Peabody."

Red chose the latter. A few minutes later, he pulled into a parking spot in front of the Peabody. Luckily, it was under a street light, so we had enough lighting for him to see what I had. One by one, I handed the articles to him, until he accumulated the pile in his lap.

"Death Captures Crown of Rock and Roll; Elvis Dies Apparently After Heart Attack," *Commercial Appeal,* August 17, 1977

"A Lonely Life Ends on Elvis Presley Boulevard," *Press-Scimitar*, August 17, 1977

"KING ELVIS DEAD," *The Sun,* August 17, 1977

"Elvis the Untold Story," *National Enquirer*, September 6, 1977

The *National Enquirer* cover contained the now-legendary photo of Elvis in his coffin. It still disturbed me to look at it, and it seemed to have a similar effect on Red. When I handed him a photo of the funeral procession, with the incredible crowds of fans lining Elvis Presley Boulevard, he said quietly, "You can't do this to me Maggie. You just can't."

That made my eyes water, but before the tears flowed, I handed him another photo of the Memphis Mafia carrying Elvis' casket at the cemetery. Red sucked air. "Don't do this, Maggie, please don't!" Pall bearers Jerry, Joe, George, Lamar, Billy, Gene and Dr. Nick were pictured. "Oh, God! Where am I? Where am I, Maggie? Am I dead, too? Holy Christ!"

I reached out to touch his hand. "No Red, no, you're not dead. You're very much alive. It's just …" my voice trailed off.

Red looked me in the eye. "Just what? Why am I not at Elvis Presley's funeral?"

"Because …" I pulled a tissue from my purse and wiped my nose. "Because you guys had a falling out, near the end of his life. You were trying to get him to make changes, to stop taking pills, to improve his health. He didn't like that. He didn't want you around anymore. Elvis fired you, Red. I'm so sorry." This was hurting me so much, the sadness of it all and not knowing if I was doing the right thing in telling Red.

He whipped his car door open and got out. I scurried to pick up the papers that fell off his lap to the seat and the floor. I got out of the car and went around to the driver's side, grabbing a clipping that had fallen into the street. Keeping an eye on Red, I tucked them back into the envelope until there were no more visible signs of the proof I'd promised him.

Red was staring off in the distance. "We need to make this quick. We need to get back before Elvis starts wondering." He turned to make eye contact. "Let's go. Now." He headed toward the hotel entrance.

"Red," I called after him, following him inside the main lobby.

He turned and shushed me. "Enough. Go get what you need and get back down here. Elvis said to hang on to our rooms for a couple more nights, in case we need them." With that, he walked toward the front desk.

I took the elevator to the 9th floor and let myself into the room I had with Grace. I ran to the bed and threw myself upon it to cry. I pulled myself together quickly, though, and packed pajamas, cosmetics and a change of clothes into our tote bag. I left the room and headed back down to the lobby.

The ride back to Graceland was even more quiet, but I wasn't finished. I had more to say. Eventually, I gathered the courage. "This is bad, sad, scary stuff, Red, but it's true. I know I've hurt you and I'm really, really sorry." I looked over at him. "Maybe we can use this information to change things!"

He was shaking his head. "None of this makes any sense, Maggie. It's so hard to believe, it ought to be a science fiction movie!"

"I know, but we can possibly change things, Red," I pleaded. "Change history."

Red was quiet as he pulled the car into Graceland. The gates opened and he drove up the driveway. "My head is about to explode. I can't be around you right now." He pulled the car into its space in the carport, put it in park and looked at me. "I think, for Elvis, for me, for all of us, you and your little girl need to go back where you came from." He got out of the car and went inside the house.

I got out too, tucking the envelope into my purse. *I know you're hurting, Red, but you're not the only one.*

It was dark, yet Grace came running up to me on my way into the house. "Grace! What are you doing out here? You need to be careful in the dark," I said, looking around for her temporary guardian.

"I am, Mama." She had something in her hand. Billy was standing nearby, with a Frisbee. I nodded at him.

"What's that in your hand?" I walked up to see her better.

"A Jelly Belly bag, Mama—Uncle Mark's favorite candy!"

Oh my God. *No!* This couldn't be. Is he here? I spun around, then recovered, quickly snatching the wrapper out of Grace's hand. I didn't want Billy to get wise to anything.

"Thanks, Grace. We'll just toss it in the trash." I tried to make it a small thing, though my heart was pounding in my chest. *Is my brother here right now?* My eyes searched everywhere in the darkness.

"I miss Uncle Mark," Grace added.

I didn't see him anywhere. Was he hiding? Was he inside? *Shit!* "I know, Grace. We'll see him again soon." *Hopefully not anytime soon.*

I took Grace and our things to our temporary quarters, a four-room apartment that used to be a four-car garage. There was a living room, kitchen, bedroom and bath—much more than we needed—and I felt bad Marty was put out. Grace was tired and so was I, so we methodically got her ready for bed. I didn't have to do much coaxing and soon she was under the covers, snuggling her duck and falling asleep. I was tempted to lie down with her and call it a night, but thought I'd better rejoin the group in the basement, so as not to be an ungrateful house guest.

When I went downstairs, the movie was more than half over. I looked around the darkened room and didn't see Red. It was quiet, except for the sounds of Sinatra hijacking a train of POWs to Switzerland. Pat asked where Red was and I told her he got a headache and went to lie down. Elvis shooshed me, the second time I'd been shushed by him tonight. Priscilla was curled up with him on the couch, in a comfy sweater and pants. Pat got up and left, and I took her seat.

I tried to settle in for the rest of the movie. The Chairman of the Board was on the screen, but my mind was on Jelly Bellys. What does that found wrapper mean? Jelly beans have been around for a long time but I'm darn sure Jelly Bellys haven't. That could mean my brother came through the wormhole! Did he stay? Elvis surely had enough security that he'd be discovered if he was lurking on the Graceland property. He might get hurt, or arrested, if there's a scuffle. What's he after?

The movie ended. Everyone, other than Elvis, looked tired and ready for bed. Folks were stifling yawns. I knew his nocturnal ways were tough on his entourage; it was affirming to see it in person. I thought of an excuse to leave. As I got up, Elvis' eyes were on me. I spoke before he could, "I'm going to check on Grace. If I don't make it back, thanks for the hospitality and see you tomorrow." I looked across the room at Marty. "Thanks very much for giving up your apartment." He gave me a neutral nod of his head.

As I passed Elvis, he held up his hand and I gave him a high five. "Good night, Maggie the Moody girl." He held on to my hand for a few extra seconds, which tugged at my heart. Priscilla looked at him inquisitively.

I went back to our apartment and quietly let myself in, even though I knew Grace would be zonked out until morning. I looked at my watch; it already *was* morning. I hoped to fall asleep quickly, for what would amount to a long nap instead of a full night's rest.

I changed into my nightshirt and crawled into bed with Grace. I turned out the light and listened for the sound of her breathing. I said a prayer and drifted off. At Graceland, once again.

I was awakened by a soft kiss on my cheek. It scared me, actually. I jumped, then heard "Ssshhh." I rolled on to my back and shook the cobwebs from my mind. My eyes focused on Elvis.

"Elvis!" I said in a loud whisper and glanced at Grace beside me. "What are you doing here?" He was in a light blue satin robe and matching pajama pants.

"I can't sleep," he replied. "Come with me to the living room." He took my hand. "Please?" Slowly, quietly I got up out of bed. Still groggy, I half-stumbled behind him out of the bedroom.

"Is something wrong?" I asked him after closing the bedroom door. "Where's Priscilla?"

"She's asleep upstairs." He sat on the couch. "Come here and sit with me."

I hugged myself, chilled by being out from under the blankets. I sat down next to Elvis and he put his arm around me. He reached for the coverlet on the back of the couch and wrapped it around me, too. "Are you OK?" I asked.

"Yeah, sure, I'm fine. I ..." he paused.

I looked at him. "You what?"

"I need you right now."

This man had the ability to melt my heart at any given time. "You need me? Or you want me?"

He laughed softly. "How about both."

I smiled and leaned into him. "Elvis, I'm so tired." I thought of Chris. "Could we lie here together, and maybe you'll be able to get some rest?"

"You don't have to do a thing," he suggested. Gently, he laid me down on the couch and put a pillow under my head. He covered me with the blanket and kissed me softly on the lips. He undid the sash to his robe and took it off, letting it fall to the floor. There was Elvis, in nothing but his pajama pants. Incredibly sexy, obviously aroused. My heartbeat quickened and suddenly I wasn't so tired, or regretful, anymore.

"Kiss me," I begged. He got down on his knees in front of the couch and we kissed passionately. Before long, I was tossing aside the blanket and he was raising up my nightshirt, his hands roaming everywhere.

"You are so sexy," he whispered between kisses. "Smile for me." I gave him a curious look. "I wanna to see those dimples."

I smiled. Elvis kissed first one dimple then the other. He stood up and dropped his pants. Lord have mercy, I could feel my pulse in multiple places! He laid down next to the couch and coaxed me on top of him. We made love on the living room floor. Once again, I was filled with ecstasy and enchantment. It was beautiful and lasted longer this time. Forever would have been fine with me.

We snuggled on the floor afterward. Elvis was relaxed and drifting off to sleep. My brain took over and started to assess the scene.

"Elvis," I whispered, "you're sleepy now, you can go back to your bed."

"I wanna stay here," he replied, in a baby-talk kind of voice.

That'll go over really well with Priscilla. "Well, at least get up on the couch and let me cover you up." As he got up, I helped him back in to his pajama pants. We couldn't risk a naked Elvis Presley here when Grace woke up. I covered him with the couch blanket and his robe, too, thinking he might put it back on when we woke up. I kissed him on the forehead and did the right thing—I headed back to the bedroom to sleep next to my daughter.

So much to think about. I'm so tired. Elvis has the power to pull me away from Chris. He has the advantage, too—he's here and Chris is not.

CHAPTER 24

Wheels on My Heels

Grace and I slept in, much later than usual, so we must have needed it. Sleep was a precious commodity at Graceland, where the plot was thickening.

Grace awakened me with a kiss on my cheek, then climbed on top of me. “Mama,” she said softly. “I have to go potty.”

That got my brain in gear. We were not at home where she could find her way by herself. I sat up quickly. Was Elvis still asleep on the couch? The bedroom door was closed. I looked at the clock on the nightstand. It was 10:15 a.m. “How did you sleep?” I asked her.

“Like a Peabody duck!” she exclaimed in her cute, husky morning voice, holding up her new animal.

I got out of bed and opened the door, peeking out into the rest of the apartment. No sign of Elvis! Back in the room, I spotted a robe on the dresser and wondered how it got there. Maybe one of the maids had brought it for me? I put it on and motioned to Grace. “C’mon, we have our own bathroom in this little apartment.” We headed into the bathroom located just outside the bedroom.

After we were finished, we changed Grace into a more casual outfit: dark pink stretch pants and a striped long-sleeve mock turtleneck with horizontal stripes in three shades of pink. Feeling a little rebellious, I stayed in my robe. I knew Elvis didn’t allow Priscilla to roam the house in hers. But he did, as I remembered his surprise seduction.

“Are you hungry, baby? Wanna go see what’s cooking in the kitchen?”

“Alberta’s cooking in the kitchen! I want breakfast, Mama!” I took her hand and we headed across the house.

"Well, look who's awake, our little guest of honor!" Alberta said to us over the sounds of the quaint, short order operation.

"Good morning, Alberta. Good morning, everyone," I greeted the room. There were a couple others—Dodger and Marty—having coffee and morning grub, which smelled wonderful.

"Miss Alberta, I'm so hungry I could eat an elephant. May I please have some breakfast?" Grace asked, getting a couple of laughs at her sense of humor.

"Miss Grace, I can make you eggs and bacon, or cereal and cinnamon toast, but I ain't cooking no elephant!" She laughed heartily. "This kitchen ain't big enough!"

Grace giggled. "I wouldn't really eat an elephant. I was just teasing." I lifted her up into a seat while Albert poured me a mug of hot coffee.

"What sounds good, baby?" Alberta asked her.

"Cereal and cinnamon toast!" Grace replied. Looking at me, she added, "Please. And thank you."

"Cereal and cinnamon toast it is." Alberta got to work on Grace's breakfast order.

"Mama, that's Elvis' grandma, Minnie Mae," Grace pointed out.

"Hello, Dodger. I mean, Minnie Mae," I didn't know if she would remember me from years ago, when she told me to call her Dodger. "It's nice to see you."

"Why did you call her Dodger, Mama?" Grace asked.

"That's what Elvis calls me, so you can, too, missy," Dodger replied.

"Are you still his grandma?"

"Yes, indeed, honey, yes, indeed."

After serving a plate of breakfast to Grace, Alberta asked, "What can I get for you, Miss Maggie?"

"I'm going to be bad and have some of your biscuits and gravy. And bacon," I replied.

"What could be bad about that?" She laughed. "Coming right up."

After our tasty Graceland breakfast, Grace and I went back to our temporary quarters. While there wasn't anything going on, I decided to give her a bath, and myself a shower. I had no idea what our plans would be so I put Grace back in the pink play clothes and for me, it was another pair of stretch pants—these with a black and white houndstooth pattern—and a long-sleeve black mock-neck sweater.

When we finished, we ventured back to the house to see if anything was going on. It was still relatively quiet. Here and there, Alberta and Mary cleaned and dusted. I didn't want Grace to make noise or get wound up, so we headed back to the apartment for some quiet time.

I didn't have any of her story books to read, so I made up a story about a Peabody duck who wandered away from the hotel and his family. Luckily, Grace got drowsy. I figured a nap would do her good. I snuggled her up in a blanket. "Mama, when do I get to see Elvis and Priscilla?" she asked.

"After your nap," I replied, and began running my fingers through her hair. "I love you, Amazing Grace."

"To infinny and beyond, Mama Llama." She was asleep in a few minutes.

While she dozed, I snuck away to see what might be happening. Elvis had awakened and was eating in the dining room. Word had spread that he indeed wanted to ride motorcycles out to Mud Island. I heard Marty say that Elvis was a little cranky since he was up earlier than usual. I also knew that he had less rest because of his sneaky, nocturnal visit.

Preparations were underway, with people coming and going. I wanted to go on the ride, too, but with Grace asleep, was unsure if I'd be able to. When I went to look out the front door to watch folks scurrying, Elvis spoke up from the dining room. "Maggie, you're coming with us." He was already dressed in off-white pants and jacket, with an olive green mock turtleneck.

"I don't know how to ride a motorcycle," I said.

"Ha!" he laughed. "Very funny. You'll be in the bitch seat."

"Excuse me?"

"Aw, c'mon, honey, lighten up. You're gonna ride with one of the guys."

I rolled my eyes at him and he winked back—the dog. "Grace is asleep in the annex, so I'm not sure."

"Alberta can watch her," Elvis said, decisively.

"She'll be afraid if she wakes up and I'm not here.

"I said Alberta will handle it, Maggie. Don't be ungrateful."

Whoa! Someone *was* cranky! I decided not to make his mood worse and shut my mouth. I went outside and looked around for possible escorts. Priscilla, obviously, would ride with Elvis. There were other girls hanging around, so I had no idea who I'd be assigned to, but a bike ride sounded fun anyway.

Jerry came up behind me, interrupting my thoughts. "May I take you for a ride today, Maggie?" he asked.

I was a bit surprised by his invitation; Jerry got banged up in a motorcycle accident earlier this year in California. I wondered aloud if he was up to it. "Sure, Jerry, but … are you back on the bike, after your accident?"

"Oh, yeah, sure," he replied, like it was no big deal. "I figure, when you fall down, you just have to get back up and try again."

"Literally," I said, with a laugh. "I'd love to be your riding partner. Let me run inside and make sure Alberta will be OK to watch Grace, since Grace will undoubtedly wake up before we get back. And I'll put on something warmer."

"Sounds good. I'll bring a bike jacket for you, too. See you soon."

This ought to be fun—a 23-year old Elvis bodyguard and a cougar.

Back in the house, I sought out Alberta. I found her in the kitchen, putting dirty dishes in the sink. "Alberta, the group is going on a bike ride and Elvis insisted I go, and said you would keep an eye on Grace. She's napping in the annex now, and I'm a little worried she'll be afraid when she wakes up alone and I'm not here."

"Don't you worry, Miss Maggie, I'll go sit with her after you leave." Motioning to the sink, she added, "I got dishes to do, but maybe I'll get a cat nap until she wakes up, then bring her 'round to help me."

"Oh, thanks, Alberta! She'll love helping you do the dishes. Tell her Mama will be back soon."

"I sure will. If Miss Grace and I have enough time, we'll bake a fresh batch of cookies!"

"She'll really love that! Thanks again." I left the kitchen and went back to our annex apartment. Grace was fast asleep. Yesterday was a long day for her. My wardrobe was limited but I hadn't yet worn the black and white houndstooth button-down vest that goes with the outfit I had on, so I added it for an extra layer. I blew her a kiss from the doorway as I left.

It was a beautiful autumn day. The sun was shining; the sky was blue. The guys revved the engines of their bikes. I heard Joe say he had to get used to the feel of his Memphis bike again after riding his West Coast bike all year. I marveled at the fact that Elvis had two fleets of motorcycles, one for each side of the country.

Elvis was astride his new brand new 1966 Harley-Davidson FLH and it was a beauty—blue and white with saddle bags, buddy seat and windshield. "Where's Red?" he asked, over the noise.

"He's in bed with a bad headache," Marty replied. "Pat's going to stay back, too." *Oh no!* That could be my fault.

On my way to Jerry, I passed Elvis. "Did you do something to Red last night?" he asked.

I didn't see Priscilla nearby. "Did you do something to *me*?" I whispered back.

Jerry handed me a bike jacket. "It's a bit big," he said, "but it will keep you warm." I noticed Elvis' eyes were on us as I put on the jacket and zipped it up.

We were soon on our way down the long Graceland driveway and out on to Highway 51. There was a nip in the air, which felt even chillier as the wind started whipping me. I ducked behind Jerry for a little more warmth. Sensing my reaction to the cold, he said, "Put your, arms around me. We'll get some body heat going." I snuggled up behind the guy who was Elvis' body double in the movies.

Our motorcycle caravan headed downtown, to the Mississippi River shoreline. I could see Mud Island—it was just a few hundred feet away—but couldn't figure out how we were going to get there. Today, visitors take a monorail, suspended from a cable over the river, to get to Mud Island River Park and its attractions.

Before I could ask Jerry, the lead bikers, Elvis and Marty, pulled up to a large pontoon boat. Everyone else followed. "We're taking that to Mud Island? All of us?" I asked Jerry, over the noise of our brigade.

"Yep, it's the ferry to the airport," he replied.

It was then that I saw a sign: Memphis Downtown Airport. "There's an airport out there?"

"Yeah, it's been an airport for a few years now."

"How are we going to get around that? Planes taking off and landing?" I wondered if Elvis had ordered another phone call to gain special permission.

Jerry read my mind. "You know Elvis. He's got connections."

"Of course, he does."

When the ferry was ready for us, we climbed off the bikes and one by one, the guys walked them down the ramp and on to the pontoon. The girls and I followed; I smirked at the idea that we were a bunch of biker bitches. The crew was attentive, no doubt surprised by their famous passenger.

It was a chilly ride across the water, the river winds whipping us. Jerry came up and put his arm around me. "More body heat?" I asked.

"More body heat," he agreed. I put my arm around him, too, and looked over at Elvis, who was shielding Priscilla from the wind. His eyes were on us. "It's a lot colder than Hawaii. Where Sandy is." He directed those comments to Jerry, and I felt Jerry loosen his grip around me.

"Don't you worry," I said to Jerry, the noise of the boat and wind covering me. "I have no intention of getting between you and your girlfriend." I knew that Jerry was head over heels in love with a beautiful Hawaiian girl, Sandy Kawelo, whom he'd met while working for Elvis in Oahu during the filming of *Paradise, Hawaiian Style*.

"Thanks," he replied. "I miss her something awful."

"I'd like to hear all about her sometime." If my memory was correct, Elvis would buy Jerry a ticket to Hawaii, to return to Sandy and grow their relationship. They would eventually marry.

We neared Mud Island in no time. The distance was about a football field's length. The crew swiftly docked us and prepared the ramp for departure.

"They say this island was formed around a sunken Union gunboat, after a Civil War battle," George said. I didn't point out that it was actually a peninsula.

"I heard the island would come up like a sandbar whenever the river was low," Sonny said. "Then one time, it popped up to stay."

"Mud Island … we get it up for you," Billy added.

"Good one, Marble Eyes!" Elvis laughed. What a nickname.

This time around, the crew assisted us girls up the ramp first. Then, one by one, the guys walked the motorcycles up the ramp to Mud Island. We had to be a strange sight, though no one was around to see us except the ferry crew.

"My uncle and his family spent the Depression squatting on this island," Sonny said. "Didn't make a whole lot of sense. Their farms flooded every year and their homes were on stilts."

We climbed back on the bikes and fired them up. It was a gorgeous day. I missed Grace and hoped she was behaving with Alberta, but was definitely in the mood for a ride.

The group, led by Elvis, headed out in a line of guys and girls, chrome and wheels. We rode around for a while, enjoying the sights and sounds, the sun on our cheeks. The Memphis Downtown

Airport had a long runway, like several football fields, and I soon figured out that in Elvis' world, that translated into a drag strip.

When Elvis got bored with riding at a normal speed, he and the guys unloaded their passengers and worked out a plan for some drag racing. Though I'd climbed off Jerry's bike, he stayed back a bit from the rest of the group. I felt sorry for him; I bet he didn't want to race, but also didn't want to disappoint his boss.

"You comin' with us, Jerry?" Elvis asked.

"Um, no thanks, E," Jerry replied, with hesitation. "I'm going to sit this one out."

Elvis looked as though he understood. "Too soon after the accident?"

"Yeah." Jerry replied. "I'm sorry," he added, looking down at the ground.

"Sure, man, I understand." Elvis revved his engine. To the other guys, he shouted, "Let's go!"

Elvis was competitive, and a daredevil. The other guys followed suit. The girls were huddled up as spectators. I wasn't sure I could watch; I noted not one of the guys was wearing a helmet. I turned my attention to Jerry, curious about the details of his accident. "You were in a motorcycle accident?" I asked.

"I was. A few months ago, in California."

"What happened?" Thinking he may not want to relive it again, I added, "Or maybe you don't want to talk about it."

"It's OK. I wrecked a new Triumph Bonneville 750, and nearly wrecked myself." He laughed.

"That's not funny."

"I was just thinking about how Elvis is full of surprises. I'd saved up for the bike, you see. Living in California weather had given me the urge to ride. I financed the bike—on my own—and after Elvis saw it, he bought one for himself … and the rest of the guys!"

"Unfortunate timing." I laughed a little, too.

"Yeah, well, you know Elvis. It wasn't more than a few days later I found out from the dealership he'd gone and paid off my loan."

"Amazing! And generous." A pause. "I'm sorry you wrecked it."

"Yeah. We were filming *Frankie and Johnny* and I had to be at the studio before Elvis, so I took my bike. The roads were wet and I was being careful, but this woman didn't see me when she went to turn and I ran into her, flew off my bike and over the top of her car. Landed flat on my back."

"Oh my God! You could have been …"

"I know. Paralyzed or dead." He shook his head at the memory. "Two weeks in the hospital with internal injuries. Lots of pain, got me really down. And made me realize I wasn't super human."

"Wow. I'm surprised you're back on a bike at all."

"Yeah, well, I'm physically recovered, for the most part. Still dealing with some pain. And I still have flashbacks."

"I shouldn't have brought it up. I'm sorry about that."

"No problem. We're on a bike ride, after all."

"But good call not to go drag racing today!"

He smiled. "No kidding."

We watched the guys race each other on the runway. It was very loud. Elvis always won. Nobody wiped out, thank goodness. Jerry told me a little more about Sandy. She had recently visited him in LA for a couple of weeks, where they realized they were in love. He hoped that she would be able to move to Memphis next year, so they could begin a life together. I really enjoyed this time with Jerry. He was a kind, sweet, good-looking young man.

When Elvis declared the drag races over, the guys rejoined the rest of us and we all climbed back on the bikes for the return ride home. Elvis seemed like he was in a pretty good mood. Priscilla held him tightly; I was holding on to Jerry. What a difference a few hours make.

At the musical gates of Graceland, Elvis didn't stop to greet the fans who had gathered, but he did give them a wave. We motored through and up the long driveway. When we reached the top, there was a shocking sight to see: Grace was standing on the front porch, holding hands with … my sister! My heart skipped a beat. *Good God! What is Sarah doing here?*

"Mama, Mama! Alberta and I made sugar cookies! And Aunt Sarah's here!" she shouted over the noise of the bikes. *She used the wormhole. It was working!*

Elvis looked at me. I looked at Sarah. She shrugged and gave me a "what did I do" look.

Little sister, don't you, I thought.

CHAPTER 25

Little Sister

"Maggie!" she said, coming to me. She looked beautiful, in a dark orange floral "June Cleaver" shirt-waist dress with full skirt. I hopped off of Jerry's bike, forgetting to thank him for the ride.

"Sarah!" We embraced. "What are you doing here?" I asked, casually, trying to recover some of my shock because we had an audience, including Elvis.

"You … called me, remember?" She looked at me like she needed help with her story.

I joined in the ruse. "Oh! Yes. Sorry. I invited you to come and meet Elvis." That wasn't going to make things any better. I look around at the group. "Oh my gosh. Where are my manners? Everyone, this is my sister, Sarah. Sarah, this is Elvis. And everyone. Priscilla, Jerry, Joe and Joan, Marty, Sonny …" I stopped naming names because I couldn't remember all of the girls' names.

Pleasantries were exchanged. Sarah was mesmerized by Elvis. "It's so nice to meet you, Elvis. You're even more handsome in person." Grace giggled. Sarah looked at me. "Maggie, um, I need to talk to you for a minute?"

The guys broke away to tend to the bikes, lining them up in a nice row in the carport. When Jerry passed me, I reached out and touched his arm. "Thanks for the ride, Jerry. It was fun, and nice to get to know you better."

He smiled. "Likewise, Maggie."

Elvis saw our exchange, and I added remorse to my feelings about this day. I walked up to him and Priscilla. "I'm sorry. It was bold of me. Too bold. I should not have contacted my sister about coming to Graceland." Looking at him, I added, "I hope you'll forgive me."

"Are there any more of your family members you want to invite to *my* home?" He had a devilish look in his eye—part serious, part amused.

I flushed. "I'm sorry. I should have known better." I was so embarrassed I could have run right back to the wormhole.

"Aw, what the hell." He looked around and asked, "Are there any little girls here who deserve a golf cart ride for good behavior?"

Grace raced toward Elvis. "Me, me, me!" When she reached Elvis, she looked back at me, inquisitively. I nodded my approval. She began hopping up and down. "Yay!"

"Have fun, honey. And Elvis," I added, covering my tracks in case Priscilla thought I was calling her man honey. "Be careful."

"Hop on up, Gracie," Elvis said, giving her a little boost into the front seat of a grey golf cart parked near the carport. He climbed in the large front seat, covered in a dark leather. "Scooch over a little closer to me so I can keep an eye on you. I don't want to lose any cargo." Grace smiled and did as she was told.

"You!" I said to my sister, my mood escalating as soon as Elvis and Grace drove away. The others started trailing back into the house, leaving me alone with my sister.

"It's really good to see you, sister, and thank goodness I found you." There was a new look of horror on her face.

"What's wrong?" I asked. "How was … getting here? What's going on at home? Is Chris looking for us?"

"Slow down. One thing at a time." She took a deep breath. "First of all, holy crap! I just found your wormhole and traveled through it! And met Elvis Presley!"

"You're right! How was the wormhole. I'm glad it's still working because …"

"Because why?"

"Because I think it's time for Grace and me to come home."

"What happened? Did you tell Elvis? What does he think of Grace?"

I laughed. "Now, you … one thing at a time."

"OK. You go first." We both said this simultaneously, resulting in more laughter.

"How did it go, arriving here?" I began.

"It was good. Quick. Just like you described. I'm glad I paid attention when Mark disclosed where the wormhole was that night when he was so drunk. I had to get to Memphis, and *here,* before …"

"Before what?" I interrupted.

She paused. "Before Mark does."

"Mark is coming here?!"

Sarah took my hands in hers. "He's kind of on a crusade. He's adamant that Chris is Grace's father. He got angry when I told him you knew that he found the wormhole and went back to Graceland."

I groaned. "Sarah! Why did you tell him?"

She ignored the question. "Maggie, he's coming after Elvis …"

"What?! Why?"

"He wants to prove whether Elvis is Grace's father."

"Oh my God." I was shocked. "He can't do that." Suddenly, I remembered the Jelly Belly wrapper. Mark has been here. *He may be here now.* "What if he's already here?" I looked up at the house.

"We have some time. I got a head start. He was still in St. Louis when I left."

"This is terrible! He can't just show up here. *You* can't just show up here." My current state of affairs was sinking in. My knees started trembling.

"Calm down, sis. We can figure this out." She paused, thinking. "When Grace gets back, we could grab her and leave. Go back home while the wormhole is working. Get back there before Mark gets here."

"I need to sit down," was all I could say.

Elvis drove Grace around the property. He didn't drive recklessly like he usually did when goofing around with the guys. Grace was quiet at first, wide-eyed with the experience.

"What do you think of this place?" Elvis asked her, grinning at her childlike wonder.

"It's so big. And so pretty," she replied. "Most people don't live in places like this. I love Graceland. I wish I lived here, too."

"Oh, you do, do you? But … wouldn't you miss your home?"

Grace thought about that for a moment. "Yes. I would miss my room and my dolls and my toys. And Poppy." She paused. "Maybe we can just come here on vacation?"

Elvis had cocked his head at the mention of Poppy. Distracted for a moment, he recalled Grace's question. "Vacation? We might be able to arrange something like that." He paused, then added, "Tell me about Poppy."

Grace spoke freely. "Poppy is my dad. His real name is Chris but Mama says I started calling him Poppy when I was a baby." Elvis fidgeted on the seat. "Poppy's fun. And funny. He comes to my tea parties sometimes." That made Grace giggle.

"Tea parties?" Elvis asked. "I thought tea parties were for girls."

Grace giggled again. "Well, they are, but some of my dolls are actually boys so Poppy can come, too." She was quite sure of that. "We have tea parties for boys AND girls," she added, with emphasis.

"Sounds like fun."

Sarah and I moved to the Meditation Garden to sit on a bench. I was shaking.

"We could take Grace and leave the property," Sarah said, still suggesting ideas for our situation. "Go back to your hotel or someplace. Mark wouldn't know where we were and maybe he would just turn back around."

"Not if he's after something," I disagreed. "You know him. If he's coming here to confront Elvis, we have to be here to prevent it from happening."

"OK. We'll stay here at Graceland. We'll find an excuse to hang around outside the house in case Mark arrives."

My mind was racing through scenarios. "This is so dumb, Sarah! If Mark wants to prove who Grace's father is, why doesn't he just do a test with Chris? He doesn't need to time travel!"

"He said he talked to Chris about a paternity test and Chris refused. Chris said he didn't need science to prove what he already knew—that Grace was his."

"Oh, Chris," I said, my heart breaking a little bit at the mention of his name. All of this was so unfair to him.

"Mark said he was going to get a DNA sample from Elvis. What would that be … hair?"

"They don't have DNA testing in the 1960s!"

"Then he's probably planning to grab and go. You know, get a sample here and take it to a future lab?"

"Sarah, this cannot happen! Mark is *really* sticking his nose where it doesn't belong!" I put my head in my hands. "What have I done?"

"Take a few deep breaths," she encouraged. "We'll think of something." A pause. "How has Gracie been with all of this?"

I smiled. "She's wonderful. Having the time of her life, actually." Thoughts of Grace slowed my heart rate a bit.

"How did it go … with Elvis and Grace?"

"I don't know where to begin. We don't have time for details now, but it went well. There was some drama around it, of course, but she's crazy about Elvis and I think he's smitten with her. I mean, they're out on a golf cart ride together right now." I made a broad-sweeping motion with my arm.

Elvis pulled the golf cart to a stop near the guard shack down front. "I almost forgot," he said, looking at Grace.

"Forgot what?" Her big blue eyes were quizzical.

"We're not alone," Elvis replied.

Grace looked both ways and back at him. "It seems like we are," she whispered, shrugging her little shoulders and scooting a bit closer to him and the protection he offered.

"I need to take a look inside the guard shack," Elvis added and hopped out of the golf cart.

"I'm scared!" Grace whimpered. "Don't leave me alone!"

"It's OK, honey, I'm right here and this will just take a second." Elvis quickly darted to the shack, opened the door, stepped inside, then back out with one arm behind his back.

"You see," he said as he walked the very short distance back to the golf cart. "We're not alone, because of this guy!" He produced a little white bear and presented it to Grace.

"A teddy bear!" she shrieked. "Is this your teddy bear, Elvis? Because you have that teddy bear song!" She started singing the lyrics.

"This teddy bear is tired of living in a shack and searching for someone special to take him home. Now that I know about your tea parties, I've decided the perfect person for him to go home with is you."

Grace gladly took the little bear in her arms and gave him a rightful bear hug. "Oh, he's so cute! And soft! Thank you, Elvis." Looking at him and lowering her voice, she added, "Thank you very much."

That cracked Elvis up. "Gracie, you are one amazing girl." He put his arm around her as he turned the golf cart around to head up the hill.

"That's because I'm Amazing Grace!"

"Yes, you are. And this has been one of my favorite golf cart rides."

"Mine, too," Grace agreed. "Actually, I think this is my *first* golf cart ride." She giggled, her left dimple on full display. That just made Elvis' grin all the wider.

"Here's what I've been thinking about," I said to Sarah. "Should I stay or should I go."

"Isn't that a song?"

"Be quiet and listen," I admonished. "I need your help."

"We don't know exactly how much time is passing in the future while we're here in the past. It's very unfair to Chris that Grace and I left under false pretenses. It's also not fair to Elvis and Priscilla that I'm here. I'm not saying that I have the power to break them up, but it can't help that I'm around." I paused, thinking about how lust and temptation overtook him last night.

"Yeah, I'm sure Lisa Marie would appreciate being born."

"She will be. Elvis and Priscilla are destined to be together. Grace is destined to live in the time she was born in. I have to do what is best for her. She deserves to be raised by her Poppy. Chris does not deserve my infidelity."

"He's a good man. He loves you."

"I love him. And I care deeply about Elvis. Sarah, I could kick myself for creating this mess! Elvis has been putting on a brave face, having a good time, pretending everything is fine. But he's troubled by this; I can see it in his eyes. He's already responsible for the livelihoods of so many people. I can't burden him further. I introduced him to Grace, but I can change things."

"Sounds like you made your decision."

"Yep," I agreed. "We're going home to Chris. I just need to figure out how and when, without affecting anything else."

"Or breaking any hearts," Sarah added.

The sounds of "Teddy Bear" being sung by the artist who took it to number one and his little companion could be heard on the Graceland grounds. At one point, Grace stopped singing and gazed at Elvis as he sang. When he finished, she said, "I think I like you singing that song live more than recorded."

"Oh, you do!" Elvis said, laughing. "And why is that?"

Grace shrugged her little shoulders and thought a bit more. "Because when you sing it live, I can look at you, and it makes the song better than YouTube."

"You Tube?" Elvis inquired. "What's a You Tube?"

"It's a channel on the computer. You type it in, then you type in a video you want to watch, like 'Elvis Presley,' and then you watch it!"

Elvis was quiet for a moment. "Computers and You Tube. Gracie, you have quite an imagination."

"I do like to play imagine, but they're real. If we were at my house, I could show you, but we'd have to go back through the wiggly worm and I don't like it."

Elvis cocked his head to the side, with a curious look. "Wiggly worm?"

Grace continued. "It's how we got to Graceland. Mama said she had to take me somewhere important and we went to Memphis and got a hotel room. Then we went outside the hotel room and Mama picked me up and told me it might tickle my tummy. And then we were at Graceland! My head felt spinny. But Mama said we had to go to another hotel and that's where I got to see the Peabody ducks!"

Elvis was mystified, and curious about exactly where Maggie and Grace came from. He thought it was St. Louis, but wasn't sure. "What am I gonna do with you, Little One?"

He tickled her and she giggled.

"You could," she began, holding her new bear out to him, then singing, "Let me be, your teddy bear!"

Elvis laughed and the two of them sang the rest of the way back to the carport.

CHAPTER 26

Good Rockin' Tonight

"Let's go jam in the music room," Elvis announced to those of us gathered in the kitchen. He'd come in through the back door with his little friend trailing behind. Sarah and I had come in from the Meditation Garden and were eating Alberta's delicious fudge cookies at the counter. Chocolate could cure anything, though for me it was just a temporary fix. I had troubling thoughts and pending actions.

"Jam?" Grace asked, taking his hand when they got into the room. "What's a jam?"

"Music, Gracie. Singing with you got me in the mood for some more." To Richard in the kitchen, he directed, "Round up the guys. Tell Charlie to grab a few guitars." Richard left to do as instructed. Elvis eyed Sarah up and down.

"What's that you've got, Grace?" I asked, noticing a little teddy bear.

"A teddy bear, Mama! Elvis gave him to me on our golf cart ride. He was living in the shack and needed someone to love him." With that, she brought her new bear in close for a hug.

"Thanks, Elvis, that was very nice of you," I said, giving him a smile.

"Well, your little one spins some good stories about tea parties and Poppy … and You Tube?" he replied, a bit of a question in his voice.

Uh oh. Covering, I said, "Yes, she has an active imagination."

Lowering his voice, he added, "I especially like the one about the 'wiggly worm.'"

Oh crap. I gave a fake laugh. "Yeah, that's a good one." *I've got to get us out of here.*

To Sarah, he said, "Let's go jam, Little Sister," then left the kitchen with Grace at his heels, singing the words to "Teddy Bear."

Sarah was giddy—Elvis had spoken directly to her. "Do you think he'll sing the song, 'Little Sister'?" she asked me.

I didn't need to answer. "Yes, we will! Now, get your butts in here," was Elvis' reply from the hallway.

We got up and headed to the music room, as instructed.

Elvis went straight to the piano and played "My Girl" by The Temptations. Grace sat on the piano bench beside him as he sang and joined in on the "my girls."

"Utterly adorable," Sarah whispered to me. My smile was a cover for my internal drama. We grabbed some space on a small couch.

Around us, the guys were gathering and setting up instruments. Billy prepped a snare drum and Mike brought an amp forward from a corner of the room and plugged in the guitars.

"This is so exciting!" Sarah whispered to me. I wondered silently if this would be my final Elvis Presley jam.

Sticking with Motown, Elvis played The Four Tops' "I Can't Help Myself (Sugar Pie Honey Bunch)." Sonny sat on a short stool and started keeping the beat. Charlie strummed a guitar.

"Where the hell is Red?" Elvis asked, when the song ended.

Grace sucked air. "That's a bad word!"

"Grace," I interrupted, wanting to keep the peace for as long as possible.

"Sorry, honey," Elvis said to Grace. Looking back at the guys, he asked, "Where in the *heck* is Red?"

"Still nursing his migraine," Joe answered.

"He still has a headache?" Elvis asked. "What the hell—I mean heck—happened to him? I bet Maggie had something to do with it." He turned his focus to me: "You were with him last night." That sounded terrible; I was glad his fiancée wasn't in the room. I tried to keep my even-keeled expression. "Why doesn't someone go and check on him. He ain't doin' any good lying in bed all damn-darn day," he added, catching another curse word.

Elvis moved from the piano to bass guitar and got the group started on "Little Sister." Sarah was beside herself, especially when he made eye contact with her. I, on the other hand, was getting annoyed when he looked at me during certain lyrics.

While I pouted, the guys jammed to a couple of Beach Boys hits—"Help Me, Rhonda" and "California Girls." I couldn't help but laugh, though, when Elvis did a Tom Jones impersonation of "It's Not Unusual." I thought of how many entertainers would pay tribute to *Elvis* in the future.

My mood lightened when the guys played "Mrs. Brown" and "Henry the Eighth" by Herman's Hermits. They were total goofballs, and I was impressed that they were jamming to a British band.

Charlie slowed it down a bit with Roger Miller's "King of the Road." I flashed back to childhood piano lessons when I could play that song.

After a while, Grace grew fidgety and starting wandering—touching things and climbing furniture. I kept an eye on her. Sarah returned to her priority—fashion—and asked Priscilla about her outfit: deep purple stretch pants with a bold, floral-print jacket.

"I love the colors you're wearing," Sarah said.

"Thanks," Priscilla said. "Your dress is colorful, too."

"I'm in love with today's fashions!" Sarah primped her full skirt.

"Do you want to go up and see some of my newest pieces?"

"Yes! Yes, I do!" She was ecstatic.

Priscilla looked pensively at Elvis, who had started to sing the Righteous Brothers' "You've Lost That Lovin' Feelin', a song he would eventually record and make his own. "I don't … think he would mind." Resolutely, she got up and motioned for Sarah to join her.

Grace noticed them leaving the music room. "Where are you going? I wanna go!" she said and ran up behind them.

Simultaneously, Priscilla and Sarah both reached out to take her by the hand. Grace took one of each and looked over her shoulder at me for approval. I nodded and whispered, "Behave." I returned my attention to the music.

When the song ended, Elvis said, "Guess we weren't good enough for the girls." His eyes were on me.

Embarrassed, I said, "They went to look at Priscilla's clothes."

"Women," he said, shaking his head and growing moodier.

I was sitting solo on the couch now. Jerry grabbed a tambourine and came over, sitting next to me. "We could use a little more percussion," he said, handing the instrument to me.

I hesitated. I wasn't in the mood to goof off. Jerry sat next to me and placed a bongo drum between his legs. Our proximity to each other could escalate Elvis' aggravation.

The guys played "Mr. Tambourine Man" by The Byrds. I played my best tambourine and for a few minutes, nearly forgot my worries. Next up was "Memphis, Tennessee" and Jerry and I continued to keep the beat. "This song reminds me of Chuck Berry and The Beatles," I said to Jerry over the music.

He laughed. "Yeah, those guys recorded it, too."

Just a couple of months before this moment we were sitting in, Elvis had met the Beatles at his California home. It was the Summer of '65. I'd read several accounts and couldn't resist hearing Jerry's, so I quietly asked him what I already knew: "Were you there? When Elvis met the Beatles?"

"Yeah, it was pretty incredible."

"What was it like? I'd love to have been a fly on the wall!"

"It was pretty laid back. The Beatles were quiet at first. They really wanted to meet Elvis, but there in the moment, I guess no one knew exactly what to say until Elvis broke the ice."

"I love it! What a history-making moment—all of them together. Who did you like best?"

"They were all super nice, polite guys. And funny, especially John.

He cracked me up! And I got to play pool with Ringo."

"Very cool!"

Jerry and I hadn't noticed that the current jam had ended. Elvis was glaring at us. "Listen to you two, going on about The Beatles." His voice dripped with sarcasm at the mention of the Fab Four's name. "Looks like you're both at the wrong goddammed jam session!" Charlie played the Paul McCartney's guitar riff that began "Ticket to Ride" but stopped when Elvis gave him the evil eye.

"Sorry, E," Jerry responded immediately. "No offense," he added with eyes downcast.

Poor Elvis, not being the center of attention again. I was reaching my limit. Without even thinking, I heard myself apologizing—sort of. "I'm sorry, too, Elvis. Sorry that I can't seem to do anything right today!" I stood up, handed Jerry the tambourine and left the room. Someone played the Rolling Stones guitar riff that begins "(I Can't Get No) Satisfaction" and the next jam was underway.

Elvis Presley isn't satisfied? Well, neither am I!

CHAPTER 27

Devil in Disguise

In my fury, I went to the kitchen. I needed a few minutes to calm down before I went upstairs to fetch Grace and my sister. Luckily, the usually busy short-order kitchen was quiet. I grabbed a brownie off a stack and angrily bit into it.

Little did I know, but my outburst ended the jam session. While I counted to 10 and devoured the decadent brownie, Elvis walked into the kitchen. He grabbed a brownie, too. If I weren't so mad, I'd have laughed at the mutual stress eating.

He got right to the point. "How could you do this to me, Maggie?"

Even though I knew he'd make this about himself, I was taken aback. "Do what to you, Elvis?"

"Well, let's see," he began. "You've spent most of the day flirting with Jerry."

"What? That is not true. I ..."

"It's against the rules," he interrupted.

"What rules?"

"The rules of Graceland. Girls don't get to come here and make passes at the guys. Unless I allow it."

I was incredulous. "I wasn't making a move on Jerry, Elvis. He's in love with Sandy! That's what we talked about—that and his accident. Besides, you're the one who insisted I go on the bike ride! And it wasn't as if you were going to put *me* on your motorcycle." I paused. "I guess the rules are different for you."

He didn't acknowledge my retort. "What did you do to Red?"

"I didn't do anything to Red!"

"You left with him last night and I haven't seen him since. He's sick with some stupid headache, and should be working for me!"

I wasn't about to reveal the details of my discussion with Red, so I fabricated. "Red and I didn't get along very well a few years ago. Remember? We were just … working it out."

"Working it out. Yeah, sure."

"Elvis!"

"What!"

"You infuriate me!"

"You infuriate me, too!"

I lowered my voice. "You came into my bed last night. Now you make these false accusations. I don't understand why you're doing this!"

"I don't understand how you could do this to me! You show up here, with Grace, and interrupt things," he replied. "Interrupt my life."

Ouch. "Elvis, I didn't mean to …"

He cut me off. "You disappeared years ago, Maggie! Things have changed! I might have felt something for you once." He paused for a second. "Hell, maybe I still do. But I can't do this now—I don't have time! I have my career, and Priscilla, and all of these other people to take care of!"

That hurt. "I'm sorry, Elvis, but I'm not asking you to *do* anything. I just thought …"

He cut me off again. "Did you think, Maggie? Did you?" He shook his head. "You made me feel something for that little girl." He looked away, then back at me. "She's a great kid."

It was all I could do not to burst into tears. "Elvis …"

"She might look a little like me, might even remind me a bit of myself, but how do I know you're not trying to con me?" The fire was back in his eyes. I was shocked at his accusation. "You talk about Chris, like you're trying to hurt me or something. Well, maybe he's the *Poppy*, not me!"

"I never intended …"

"You seduced me!" Elvis accused. His tone was icy. I looked at him in horror. "Yeah, that's right. Now that I think about it, this all started when you showed up here—years ago—and had your way with me. You think you're the first woman to try and get her hooks in me?"

My shock at him wore off. "Alright, that's it," I began.

"I'm not stupid, Maggie! You can't do this to me!" He sounded exasperated. "You're making me crazy!"

Now I was angry. "You know what, Elvis? You're spoiled!" I no longer cared what he thought of what I said. "You're a beautiful, talented, generous man. But, damnit, you're spoiled! And sometimes … you act like a child! Are you even aware of that part of yourself? Of how ridiculous it is when you act that way? You're a grownup, for God's sake!"

"Do you have any idea who you're talking to?" Elvis was glowering, steaming, giving me the evil eye.

"Yes, I do. Elvis Aaron Presley. A grown man, not a child. Right now, you're behaving with less maturity than Grace!" I was unafraid of the consequences of my yelling. "My God, it's as if you need to be put over someone's knee and spanked!" I made a beeline for the door. In the doorway, I turned to face him and lowered my voice. "And your memory is slipping, too, because *you* were the one seducing *me* last night!"

I left the room, wanting Grace. Was she still upstairs with Sarah and Priscilla? I took the front stairs two at a time. They were in the dressing room, surrounded by clothes, hats and shoes. I held out my arms to Grace while making eye contact with my sister. "Grace, I need you to come with me now. Sarah, too." Hesitantly, Grace approached me. I picked her up and headed out of the room. In of the corner of my eye, I saw Sarah slowly place the dress she was holding on the rack. Priscilla stood frozen, doe-eyed.

"Mama, where are we going?" Grace asked.

"Home."

She fidgeted in my arms. "I don't want to go home. I'm having fun at Graceland."

We descended the front stairs. "Grace, I told you we were just coming for a visit and now it's time to go."

"Can't we stay a little longer? Please, Mama?" Grace begged.

"Grace, it's time to zip it." She knew what that meant and fell quiet.

By the time I reached the foyer, Sarah was close behind us. She followed me to the kitchen. I was aiming for the back door.

Elvis was still in his seat and my heart sank at the sight of him. "I'm still *infuriated*, Maggie," he said.

I was still angry. too. I paused in front of him. Sarah was at my heels. "We're leaving, so you'll never have to see us again," I said calmly. Grace started crying.

"Maggie!" Elvis called after us. I ignored him and figured his pride would prevent him from getting up and coming out the back door after us.

Once outside, Sarah chided, "Maggie, he's calling you!"

Suddenly, Grace shrieked. "Uncle Mark!" She struggled to get free of my arms, and I nearly dropped her.

Sarah had warned me, yet I couldn't believe my eyes. Before us stood our brother, looking like a *Star Trek* cast member in a yellow-gold V-neck sweater, black pants and boots. "Mark!" I said, too loudly. I lowered my voice. "What are you doing here?"

Grace ran to her uncle, who scooped her up. "You came, too, Uncle Mark! I missed you! Now I can show you Graceland, and you can meet Elvis Presley!"

"Gracie, girl, I missed you, too!" Mark said, wiping a tear from her cheek while locking eyes with me. "And meeting Elvis sounds good to me."

CHAPTER 28

Too Much Monkey Business

I was fuming and Mark knew it. "What are you doing here?" I asked him again.

"I came to meet Elvis Presley," he replied, nonplussed. "Isn't that why people come to Graceland?"

"Mark, I swear I'll take you out right now."

"What? Why?" Turning to Sarah, he asked, "Is this the kind of greeting you got?"

"Not exactly," Sarah answered. "But I wasn't after …"

"Ssshhh!" Mark quieted her.

I looked back and forth at them. "Sarah told me what you're after, Mark, and that's not going to happen. This all ends now. Right here!"

"Right here at Graceland. Pretty cool, huh, Gracie?" Mark said, mocking me and setting Grace back down.

"Graceland is an amazing place," Grace said. "Amazing Graceland."

"Amazing Graceland … I like that!" he said to her, hoping the subject had changed.

"Mark, I know what you're up to," I said. "But why?"

Suddenly, it wasn't just the four of us. Red came from somewhere in the yard and surprised us all. "That … is a good question," he said, his eyes switching from me to my brother.

I exhaled. Another complication. I wasn't going through any wormhole tonight and had to think fast.

"Red, this is my brother Mark. Mark, this is Red West," I said, making another awkward introduction. While the two of them shook hands, I quickly moved on. "Red, I need a favor. Would you please take us to the hotel?" To persuade him, I added, "We can talk there."

Red exhaled. "Maggie, what's going on? Where did your brother come from?" He looked at me suspiciously. "The same place as your sister?" He squinted his eyes. "The same place as you?"

"Red, I can explain." I began.

"You've said that before."

"We have to get out of here now, Red. Elvis and I …" I paused, not wanting Grace to hear all of this. I took a step closer to Red and spoke quietly. "Elvis and I had a fight and I told him we were leaving. I want to go back to the hotel and get the rest of our things. I need to talk to my brother. *We* can talk to my brother. Please, Red."

Red glanced at Mark, Sarah and Grace. "OK. Let's take the Cadillac."

The five of us made our way to the carport. Grace started whimpering again. "I want my bear, Mama. I want my teddy bear from Elvis!" Whining turned to tears. I picked her up.

Red looked at me and I shook my head. Looking at Grace, he said, "I'll get your teddy bear, honey. Where is it?"

"I don't know." She cried harder.

"The last time I saw it was upstairs on the bed, when we were looking at Priscilla's clothes," Sarah offered.

Red made for the back door, which opened ahead of him. "I hear a little girl crying out here, what's the matter?" It was Elvis, trailed by Priscilla. Damn it all.

"I want my teddy bear!" Grace wailed.

"You can have your teddy bear! Don't cry, little one," he said to her. To the rest of us, "Where's the bear I gave her?"

"I think it's upstairs," Priscilla replied. "I'll go get it." She hurried back inside.

Elvis looked around and noticed my brother. "Aw, now what!

Who the hell is this?"

I could have died. "This is my brother, Mark. Mark, this is Elvis." A feeble introduction.

"Hey, Elvis," Mark said, and extended his hand, but Elvis didn't shake it.

Looking at me, Elvis said, "Your brother? Really? What, Maggie, are you planning a goddamned family reunion here? Where's *my* invitation?" Mark and Sarah stood frozen and wide eyed.

"No, Elvis, I'm not." I replied. "I'm sorry. This whole thing is just …"

"Just crazy, is what it is!" he interrupted. "Just crazy!"

"I know. It *is* crazy. And like I told you, we're leaving. I promise. Thanks for your generous hospitality—with Grace, with everything. I'm sorry if we … *interrupted your life*." I threw his words back at him. "It's time for us to go."

"Maybe you're right."

The back door opened again and Red came out, trailed by Sonny. How many more folks could we involve in this drama?!

To Elvis, I continued. "Red's going to give us a ride to the hotel, to collect the rest of our things, then we'll be on our way." I had yet to figure out how the four of us were going to get back to the wormhole, in this very backyard, unseen.

"All of these family members here and not one car?" Elvis asked. "Did y'all arrive on the Starship Enterprise?" He was looking at my brother's ensemble and I would have laughed if I wasn't so embarrassed. Others snickered at Elvis' joke.

"We came through the wiggly worm, right over …" Grace said, but I cut her off.

"Grace! Not now. This is not a time for stories." She knew I was serious by the tone of my voice.

Motioning to my siblings and me, Red directed, "All of you, *family members*, get in the back seat of the Caddy." We did as we were told. Sonny followed us and got in on the front passenger side. Weary of awkward introductions, I quickly introduced him to my brother.

"I got this, E," I heard Red say to Elvis outside the car, no doubt another one of his attempts at de-escalation.

Priscilla, luckily, returned with a white teddy bear in hand. She handed it to Grace through the car window.

"What do you say, Grace?" I said.

"Thanks for finding my teddy bear, Priscilla."

"You're welcome, sweetie," she replied.

"Thanks, Priscilla, for putting up with all of this nuttiness," I said to her. "I never intended for things to get so out of hand."

"It's OK," she said, looking around at the scene. "Families can be like that, sometimes." She was sweet; however, I bet she was glad to see us go.

I had one last thing to say to her. "Take care of Elvis."

She nodded. "I will."

Red got in and started the car. When he put it in reverse to back out of the carport, I realized I didn't have my purse or tote bag. "My bags!" I said. Red hit the brakes. "I need to get my purse and tote bag from the annex. Please."

Red put the car in park. I hopped out and dashed past Elvis and Priscilla to the annex. I literally threw our things into my tote, grabbed my purse and ran back out.

On my way back to the car, Elvis called out, "Watch out for this one right here! She is M-O-O-D-Y!" I didn't look at him until I was back in the car. He wore a cocky grin. *You're the moody one,* I thought. As Red drove us away, I kept my eyes on Elvis for as long as I could, wondering if it would be the last time I'd ever see him again.

"Bye bye, Elvis Presley," Grace whimpered softly, peering out the back window. "Bye, bye, Graceland." We laid her across our laps and she cuddled her teddy bear. "Do you have any Jelly Bellys?" she asked Mark. "I found an empty bag in Elvis' yard."

With me glaring at him, he replied, "No, Grace, I'm all out right now." Mark ran his fingers through her curls and she was asleep in a few minutes, exhausted from upside-down lifestyle.

When I caught Red's eye in the rearview mirror, I nodded my head toward Sonny with an inquisitive look. "Reinforcements," he said softly. Oh. I didn't realize those were needed.

It was a mostly quiet ride to the hotel. At one point, my brother whispered to me, "We need to talk."

"You better believe it, but keep your mouth shut until we get to the Peabody," I whispered back.

"The Peabody," he said, a bit louder. "Somebody's livin' it up."

"Be quiet, Captain Kirk."

Sarah snickered.

I needed a few minutes to think. I never imagined things would get so messy. I'm hurting people, including myself.

CHAPTER 29

Suspicious Minds

"That's one very strange family," Elvis said as Red drove them away. He put his arm around Priscilla; she fit so perfectly in the space beside him. "Pisses me off how they all showed up, uninvited."

"Now I know why you don't like the name Maggie. Or Moody," she said, remembering his recent outburst. "There's something wrong with her."

"You think so, Satnin? I've been trying to figure it out. I knew Maggie years ago, and she was strange then, kind of like she was out of place. I actually liked that about her; I could connect to it. But she disappeared, then showed up again after all this time … with that little girl." He paused. "I like that kid."

"She's cute."

"And funny! And clever. Like a big person in a little body—ahead of her time." Elvis fell quiet; he was thinking.

Patsy popped out of the back door, saw the two of them and headed over. "What's going on out here? The place was noisy as usual, then got quiet."

"Red and Sonny took our guests to the Peabody," Priscilla replied.

"Maggie and Grace?"

"Yes. And Maggie's sister, and brother."

"Brother and sister, oh my!" Patsy exclaimed. "When in the world did they get here? Or should I ask … how?"

Elvis snapped out of his thoughts. "What do you mean by that?"

"Oh, I probably don't mean anything. It's just that it's never been really clear how Maggie got here, this time or the first time."

"She came from St. Louis, right? Maybe she hopped off a bus right out by the gates."

"I don't mean that, Elvis." She paused. "Aw, never mind."

"No, c'mon," he pushed. "Spill it."

"Sounds interesting," Priscilla encouraged.

"Well, last night, while you guys were riding go karts around the driveway, Maggie and I talked. She wanted to explain why she suddenly disappeared from here those years ago, and …"

"Why did she?" Elvis asked. Patsy did not reply. "You can tell me, cousin."

"She said she was homesick, for St. Louis, and for …" she looked strained. "For the year 2006." She paused. "She said she was from the future."

"2006! She must be crazy!" Priscilla said, wide eyed and looking up at Elvis for his reaction.

"She told you that? That business about being from the future?" Elvis shook his head. "She told me that, too."

"Do you believe her?" Priscilla asked him. Looking at Patsy, "Do *you* believe her?"

When we arrived at the Peabody, Red pulled up to the front door and the valet approached to assist with the car. Red looked at Sonny then back at the valet. "We need to collect our things from a couple of rooms and check out. Sonny here will stay with the car." Turning to look at us in the back seat, he said, "The rest of you, no monkey business. Stick together, go up to the room and get your things, then meet me in the lobby where we'll have ourselves a little conversation."

Grace was still sleeping in our laps. Red noticed me look at her. "One of you can stay here with Grace, or lay her down where she's at and Sonny will keep an eye on her."

"It's alright, I'll carry her. She goes with us," Mark said, a bit defiant.

We all climbed out of the back seat. Mark was gentle with Grace, trying not to wake her up. We followed Red into the main lobby. When we parted ways, to the front desk and elevators, he said, "Go up, pack up and get back down here."

"Aren't you going to …" I started to ask Red about going up to collect Elvis' things.

"I'll be right behind you," Red interrupted.

While we waited for our elevator ride, Mark said, "Geez, who does he think he is, bossing us around like that?"

"Only Elvis Presley's primary security," I replied.

Sarah had noticed a little boutique inside the hotel but it was closed. "Oh, I wish I could go shopping!" Little did she know I had a surprise for her in the room.

"I'm sorry, Sarah," I said. "You've been such a good sister and this trip wasn't fair to you."

"It wasn't fair to any of us," Mark said.

"Shut up," I said.

We took the elevator to the 9th floor and the hallway to our room. I let us in and immediately began packing the rest of our items into my tote bag.

Mark laid Grace down on the bed. "Whew! Little girl was getting heavy." Sarah sat on the bed next to Grace and covered her with part of the bedspread.

"This … is for you," I said, presenting Sarah with the blue and white coat. "From Elvis, actually. He sent me to the boutique yesterday while he rested, and I picked this out for you."

"Oh, my goodness, I love it!" she exclaimed.

"Sshhh," I said, pointing to Grace on the bed. Sarah put on the coat and headed for a mirror.

"We need to talk, Mags," Mark said.

"I know! Give me a second."

He tried the doorknob to the adjoining room, and it opened. "Hey! What's this? Aren't these supposed to be locked?"

"It was Elvis' room," I replied, before realizing that maybe I shouldn't have said that.

"Elvis stayed here? Next to you? Well, all right!" Mark went into the adjoining room.

"Mark!" I said, a bit too loudly. Grace began to stir. Sarah, still in her new coat, tried to quiet her back to sleep.

He shut the door behind him. I tried the knob. He had locked it. "Mark, get back here. You're liable to run into Red when he gets up here!" No reply. "Mark, I'm not kidding!" A pause. "Please, don't mess with anything in that room!"

"Mama, who are you talking to?" Grace was awake, but groggy. "Where are we, Aunt Sarah?"

"Hey, baby! How was your nap?" Sarah replied, pulling Grace on to her lap.

"It's alright, Grace," I said. "We're back at the Peabody for a little bit."

Grace hugged her teddy bear. "Are we going back to Graceland? I wanna go back to Graceland, Mama." Looking around, she asked, "Where's Uncle Mark?"

"Take it easy, honey. You just woke up. Give Mama a few minutes." I gave Sarah a "help me'" look and she took over the soothing.

I tried the doorknob again, then knocked. "Mark? Please unlock this door."

He did, and strutted back into the room. "As you command, big sister."

"Uncle Mark!" Grace exclaimed.

"Look who's awake!" he said, and headed toward Grace and Sarah on the bed.

"Mark, tell me you didn't disturb anything in that room … didn't *take anything* from that room," I said.

He held his hands up. "Alright, I'll tell ya. Nothing in my hands!" He spun around once, hands still up. "Nothing on me." I hoped he was telling the truth.

We heard some rustling in the room next door. That had to mean that Red had come up to gather the things that Elvis had in his room. Mark looked at me then Grace. He sang, "Who's afraid of the Big Bad Wolf?" Grace giggled.

"Mark," I said. "We need to talk."

Suddenly switching tracks, he shrugged it off. "Nah, it can wait. It will be much more interesting to see what *the big, bad boss man* wants to talk about."

There was a knock at the adjoining door, then, "Maggie? You still in there? It's Red."

I opened the door and Red came through, a hotel laundry bag in his hands containing, I guessed, what Elvis had in that room.

"I'm finished packing," I told him. "Are you ready to go?"

Red looked around at all of us, including Grace. "Time to talk," he said. "Grace, what do you say we take you down to assist Sonny with automobile security?" He was concocting an opportunity for her not to be around when we spoke.

"Yes, Red West! I'm ready!" she answered. "As long as teddy bear can help, too!"

"Teddy will also be on the security team."

We all left the room and took the elevator back down to the lobby. I carried Grace and it felt good to have her in my arms, amid this evolving soap opera. "Grab that little seating area over there," Red said to us. "Grace, you come with me and we'll get you set up with Sonny."

"OK, sir!" She was ready for her assignment.

"Seriously, Maggie," Mark said as we sat on a group of comfortable chairs. "That guy needs to get over himself."

"You know, Mark, you may have made it possible for all of us to be here, but have you stopped to think about *when* it actually is?" He just stared at me. "It's 1965, and Red West is Elvis' bodyguard!" I was getting exasperated. "Look at what we've done, what we've barged into, what we've disturbed!" I almost started crying. "He has every right to behave like way!" I realized I had developed quite a respect for Red. I lowered my voice and looked back and forth at my brother and sister. "I think he believes me now. I think that's what he wants to talk about." I paused. "We need to be honest with him, and then maybe we'll be able to go home."

"Maggie couldn't really be from the future, could she? That sounds like a movie or something!" Priscilla said.

"I don't believe her," Elvis said, though not with complete certainty.

"I don't either," Patsy said. "I actually laughed when she told me." She laughed again.

"I did, too," Elvis agreed, with a chuckle.

"And that poor child," Patsy added. "Cute as all get out and what's Maggie gonna do but ruin her little mind."

"That's sad," Priscilla said.

"Let's go inside," Elvis said, and led the way. In the kitchen, the scent of bananas filled the air. Alberta had made a fresh bowl of banana pudding. "Alright!" he exclaimed and made himself a heaping bowl of his favorite dessert. He ate in silence, thinking some more. After half a bowl, he said, "Let's suppose we *did* believe her."

"What?!" Priscilla asked.

Simultaneously, Patsy reacted. "Believe who? Maggie?"

"I'm putting some things together in my mind," he began. Priscilla and Patsy looked at each other, then back at him. "When I took Grace for the golf cart ride this afternoon, she said some weird stuff. At first, I thought she was just being imaginative. You know how kids are. But now I'm wondering if there isn't something to it all."

"What did she say?" Patsy asked.

"We were singing and she said I sounded better in person than a You Tube."

"What's a You Tube?" Priscilla asked.

"That's what I asked her and she said it was a channel to watch on a computer. How is that possible? A super computer is huge and the new mini-computer costs about 20 thousand bucks."

"That *is* weird, coming from a little girl," Priscilla said.

"And there's more," Elvis continued. "She said she could show me her You Tube and computer if I'd go with her through the wiggly worm."

Patsy laughed. "Now that definitely sounds like a child's nonsense! A wiggly worm?"

"I agree, except Maggie shushed Grace a few minutes ago when she said 'wiggly worm.' Grace told me it was how her and her mama got to Graceland. Something about a hotel and a room and tummy tickling and head spinning."

Priscilla laughed. "Elvis, you were right the first time when you said she had a good imagination."

"Yeah, maybe," he said. "I can't help but feel like there's something else, though, something deeper. She's just a little kid, but combined with her mother, what's the purpose of their visit? Are they just fans, or could they really be from another time? Is it part of God's plan? What are we supposed to learn from them? I can't put my finger on it."

"I have my suspicions, too, cousin." Patsy looked at Elvis and gave a tiny nod toward Priscilla, as if to say, "not in front of her."

Elvis took the hint. "Cilla, honey, would you go up and get me my *Impersonal Life* book?"

"But …" She didn't want to miss any of this.

"No buts, baby, I need to look up a passage about fate."

Priscilla did as instructed and headed up the back stairs. As soon as she disappeared, Elvis lowered his voice and asked Patsy, "What are you suspicious about?" She hesitated. "You can tell me."

"Well, it would be one thing if Maggie showed up again, after all this time, to see you again. I could understand that. I mean, you're Elvis Presley!" She paused, choosing her words. "But she came back with that little girl. She told me she wanted Grace to know you." Again, she paused, fearing his reaction. "She told me you might be the father, Elvis. What if Maggie is trying to pin fatherhood on you?"

Elvis arched his eyebrows and sighed. "It wouldn't be the first time," he replied.

"That's true. But it has to be the strangest."

They fell quiet when they heard Priscilla coming back down the stairs. She handed Elvis the book he requested, Joe Benner's 1914 novel about self-discovery and living a spiritual life. She handed it to him and he immediately dove into the pages, which were full of his notes in the margins, highlighted passages and dog-eared pages.

Priscilla and Patsy watched him for a moment, knowing he might find what he was looking for and decide to read it aloud to them. This was a new, emerging side of Elvis—studying religions, spirituality and philosophy, searching for meaning and purpose in his life. Many in their entourage thought it was strange.

Elvis was absorbed in the book. He mumbled a few things: "God is within all" and "Is it in or out of our control?" Patsy nudged Priscilla and nodded her head toward the front of the house. Quietly, they left the kitchen.

"Maybe we should just send them on their way, when they get back," Priscilla said softly.

"Maybe," Patsy agreed. "Even if they leave, I have a feeling their footprints will be hard to remove."

In a sitting area in the Peabody lobby, Red approached us and sat in the fourth chair. For a moment, everyone just looked at each other and no one spoke. Red's eyes fixed on me. My brother asked, "Who goes first?"

"I do," Red answered immediately. "We need to get some things straight before we go back."

Mark started to speak again and I shushed him. "Mark, please!"

"I've been doing a lot of thinking," Red began. "I need to understand your motivations, why each of you showed up at Graceland, from … well, I'm not sure where yet."

"Do you believe me, Red?" I asked.

"Maggie, let me continue. Let's begin with your sister. Sarah, is it?" Sarah nodded. "Sarah, why did you come to Graceland?"

Sarah looked at me, then Mark, before answering. "I needed to tell my sister something." She looked over at the boutique windows. "And I wanted to go shopping."

"What did you need to tell your sister?"

Sarah shifted in her chair. "I think that's private, between the two of us."

"Is it?" Red asked. "I'm not sure this is the time for secrets. We're all in this mess together."

"You *do* believe me, Red!" I exclaimed.

"Maggie, hold on," he replied. Getting back to Sarah, he asked, "What did you come here to tell your sister?"

She hesitated, then replied, "I wanted to give her a heads up that Mark was on his way."

"OK. That sounds significant. Let's hear from Mark." Eying Mark, Red asked, "Why did *you* come to Graceland?"

Mark tried to play tough with Red, deciding if he would dignify his question with an answer. "I wanted to meet Elvis Presley," he replied.

"Very funny. And now for the real answer?" Red asked again.

"Mark," I interrupted. "We might as well be honest. We want to go home, right?"

Mark looked back and forth between me and Red. "I came here because of my niece, Grace," he began. "There's been some confusion, you see, and it's time to get some answers." He paused, for effect, I assumed. "We need to know the truth about Grace's paternity."

"There's a question as to who her father is?" Red asked. "Interesting. And let me guess … Elvis is one of the possibilities."

I looked at the floor, humiliated. My brother continued. "Yes. As well as another guy—Chris—from St. Louis."

Red looked at me and I blushed with embarrassment. "Is that why you came back, Maggie? To see if Elvis was Grace's father?"

"I just wanted them to know each other." I looked back down at the floor.

"It was supposed to be as simple as that," Sarah added.

Red laughed. "Simple isn't what we got."

"I'm sorry," I said.

"We're sorry," Sarah echoed.

Red looked at Mark. "How are we going to prove who the father is? I mean, good luck getting some blood out of Elvis!" He laughed again.

"We don't need blood," Mark said. "We can use DNA."

"What the hell is DNA?" Red asked.

"Deoxyribonucleic acid," Mark replied. "It's the material in our bodies that makes up our chromosomes and carries our genetic information."

"I didn't do that well in science," Red said. "It still sounds like you need his blood."

"Nope. You can get it from other parts of the body, like hair."

Hair. Oh my God—*Mark has some of Elvis' hair.* He went in to Elvis' room upstairs and took some hair.

"You need some of Elvis' hair to figure out the paternity?" Red asked.

"No, we don't," I jumped in, giving my brother a look. I bet he already had it. "Red, we need to get going. Like you said, it's time for us to go back. We've worn out our welcome with Elvis. I need to get Grace back to her regular life."

"Stay seated, all of you," he said. "There's one more thing we need to talk about."

We all eyed him anxiously. "Elvis has been hungry for education lately, and he talks about the need for an open mind, and about different levels of consciousness." He shrugged. "It's not my bag of tea, but it makes a little sense now, in this crazy situation."

He's trying to believe me. "It's my job to take care of Elvis," he continued. "He's an incredibly special person—talented, generous, funny. He's everything, and he's my boss. You," he said, pointing at me, "dropped a bomb on me with proof, should I choose to believe in that proof, that Elvis will die a young man—just 42 years old—and I," Red cleared his throat, "his bodyguard, won't even be at his funeral!"

It was Sarah and Mark's turn to look away. My eyes and ears were glued to Red. "This whole 'we're from the future' thing is impossible to comprehend, but if I have an open mind, and if you're right about Elvis' fate, well then, I've decided I have to take extra care of him, and maybe he'll live a long life."

"Oh my God, Red, yes!" I exclaimed. *He believes me!* "You can make a difference. I'm sure of it!"

"I'm not as sure as you are, but I'm gonna try. I love the guy. I'd do anything for him. And I hope to God I can avoid that 'falling out' you told me about."

"I hope you do, too, Red," Sarah said.

"Even if you don't believe us, it's still a good idea to keep an extra eye on your boss," Mark added.

"Thank you, Red. I'm sorry I hurt you, sorry for your headaches. I threw a lot at you, but understand it was out of love for Elvis. He's very special, as you said. So many people love him. Thanks for taking it all in, thinking about it and sharing your plans with us." I laughed. "We've come a long way, haven't we?"

"Yeah, we have, Maggie," he laughed, then got serious again. "Here's what we're going to do next."

Red revealed our course of action. When he was finished, we all got up and headed out the front door to Sonny and Grace waiting by the car. "Perhaps our work here is done," I said to my siblings.

"Perhaps," Mark added.

I would deal with him later.

CHAPTER 30

Get Back

It was quiet on the way back to Graceland, everyone lost in his or her thoughts. Country singers crooned on the radio. Grace, seated between her aunt and uncle, took her cue from the adults; she silently snuggled her teddy bear.

"You came through the basement?" Red asked, eyeing me in the rearview mirror. Sonny gave him a strange look.

"No, not this time," I replied, cautiously, not sure if Sonny knew what we were up to. "The backyard."

Grace, smart as a whip, added, "By the wood. The wiggly worm is by the wood."

"What the hell," Sonny said and turned around to look at Grace, at all of us.

"That's a bad word," Grace chided Sonny.

"Sorry, missy," he said. "Red, what the *heck* is going on with these folks?"

"Nothing to worry about, Sonny," Red answered. "It's just time for them to go back home."

We fell quiet again. I was grateful for my siblings' silence. Mark probably felt victorious. Sarah patted me on the knee a few times; I felt her support. Reaching into my tote bag for a pen and the little pad of paper from my hotel room, I quickly wrote a note.

I took a few deep breaths when we arrived at Graceland and the gates opened. I knew what we had to do. It was time to go home. I prayed we would be successful and return to our lives with Chris.

"Hi, Uncle Travis!" Grace yelled to the gate guard, Elvis' uncle.

"Hello there," Uncle Travis replied. "Isn't it mighty late for a little girl to be awake?"

"No, it's OK. I took a nap," Grace answered.

"Thanks, Travis," Red said and continued up the driveway. I smiled at the feeling I always get when I enter Graceland. I heard Elvis singing, "Welcome to My World" from the tours.

There were only go karts and golf carts in sight when we drove around back to the carport. "I wonder where everybody is," Sonny said.

"Probably at the Memphian," Red said as he parked us. "Why don't you go inside and take a look." Sonny obliged, opening his car door first and climbing out.

Mark spoke up. "Can I go in with Sonny and take a look around?"

I had that answer. "No! There's nothing else to see or do."

"But …" Mark interrupted.

"You've done enough, brother! We're leaving now. Before something else happens." I lowered my voice so only he could hear. "Before we're not able to anymore."

We all got out of the car. "Sarah, handle Grace for a minute."

"Sure thing."

I went over to Red. "Thank you, Red. I'll never forget you and all we've been through together. You're a good man, a good friend." I thought I saw a bodyguard blush.

"As long as I live, Maggie, and have a remembering bone in my body, you and your visits will be the strangest things I'll recall."

I laughed and handed him the note I wrote in the car. "Please give this to Elvis?" It was folded in half. Red looked at me and I nodded. He unfolded it and read it: *"Dear Elvis: Marry Priscilla. Listen to Red and Sonny. They'll take care of you. Don't let the Colonel wear you out. Love, Maggie the Moody girl."*

"It's time for us to go," I said to Red and my family. "Before Sonny gets back out here." I went and took my tote bag from Mark, strapping it across my shoulders. I took Grace from Sarah. "Let's go." I led them to the wood pile.

Grace started to cry. "I don't wanna go in the wiggly worm, Mama."

"Hush, Grace, it will be alright."

"I'm not gonna watch whatever's about to happen," Red said and turned his back to us. He assumed his bodyguard stance, legs spread slightly, arms crossed. "You got that envelope with you, Maggie?" he asked, over his shoulder.

"Yes, Red," I replied. He was referring to the newspaper stories about Elvis' death. "It's going back with me."

I lined us up while Grace whimpered. I didn't trust my brother, so he was first, followed by Sarah, then Grace with me. In a row, we inched our way behind the wood pile, hoping for the best.

The empty lot behind the Days Inn Graceland produced a pile of four people, as if from out of nowhere. Mark arrived first. "Hot damn, I still think that's freaking amazing!"

Sarah came next. "Whoa!" she exclaimed, then burst into laughter. "I feel funky!"

Grace and I brought up the rear. I was holding her in my arms, and she was crying. "I don't want to leave Graceland, Mama."

We were all disoriented as we untangled ourselves from each other and scooted away from where we landed. Sarah was the most enthusiastic. "It worked! We traveled back in time and made it back to the future!" She laughed again.

"My ears need to pop," Mark said, hitting the side of his head.

My legs felt wobbly. I sat down on a patch of grass, with Grace on my lap. "I want to play with Elvis and Priscilla at Graceland!" she cried.

"Ssshhh, Grace, it's OK. We're going home now. You'll see Poppy soon." I wondered how angry Chris was going to be.

"Sooner than you think," Mark said.

I looked his way, still furious with him. "What are you talking about?"

Mark stood up, a bit wobbly himself. "He's here. In Memphis. Should be at the hotel." He motioned to the building behind us.

"Oh my God!" I said.

"Poppy's here?" Grace jumped off my lap.

"Why?" I asked.

"I brought him with me. I figured he needed to know what was going one—where his *girlfriend* took his *daughter*—and be here when we got back."

Were it not for Grace, I would have reached out and struck him. "You," I seethed, "are a miserable, meddling fool. You have no right to interfere with our lives the way you have! When this is over …"

"This may never be over," he interrupted. I wanted to knock the smirk off his face.

"Mama, I wanna see Poppy!" Grace whined.

"Room 123," Mark said. "Across from the pool."

Still fuming, I took Grace by the hand and led her around the backside of the hotel. When I passed my brother, I whispered, "You are not my brother."

We made our way down the first-floor hallway at ground level. Chris was sitting in a chair on the pool deck, his head in his hands. The sight of him flooded my heart. It was a sunny, autumn day, though past swim season. He saw us approaching and leapt from his chair, knocking it over.

I opened the pool gate and Grace ran into Chris' open arms. He picked her up and enveloped her in a big hug. "How's my Gracie?" The look he gave me over her shoulder was mixed with emotion. "I've missed my girl," he said, studying her. "What have you been up to?"

"It was amazing, Poppy!" Grace exclaimed. "Elvis took us to Graceland! And we got to see his house and his friends. And Priscilla is *soooo* pretty. And Alberta let me cook with her in the kitchen …"

Chris' eyes darted to me, my siblings, then back Grace. "Elvis Presley? Really?"

"Yes!" Grace assured him. "It really was Elvis Presley and he was so nice. He took me on a golf cart ride and gave me this teddy bear!" She proudly showed him her little white bear.

Chris stroked Grace's curls. "Well, it sounds like you have a lot to tell me. I can't wait. But first," he looked at me, "I need to talk to your mother. Why don't you go get a snack in the room with your aunt and uncle?"

Grace, so perceptive, gave me a look of concern, as if she knew we were in trouble. She reached out and took Chris' face in her little hands. "Don't worry, Poppy. Mama and I were very careful with the wiggly worm and I behaved myself. I really did; I was a good girl." With extra emphasis, she added, "And I missed you," and gave him another hug.

"I missed you too, baby doll," Chris hugged her, then set her down in the direction of Mark and Sarah. I took the opportunity to approach him with a hug and kissed his neck. He hugged back, but there was no return kiss. Looking at me with a raised eyebrow, he said, "Wiggly worm? What is she talking about?"

Grace heard that, so she turned around and said, "The wiggly worm is how we got to Graceland, Poppy. I don't really like it because it's little scary. It makes your tummy tickle and your head gets spinny. I told Elvis about it and he said he would come visit me some day, so I don't have to miss him!" She skipped away.

I sucked air. Chris stared at me, looking perplexed and hurt. My mind swirled with the ramifications of what Grace just said. I met his gaze. Three little words had worked for me in the past. Would they now?

"I can explain."

The End

"AMAZING GRACE"

Published in 1779 by English poet/Anglican clergyman John Newton (1725–1807).

Originally entitled "Faith's Review and Expectation," the song became known by its opening phrase. "Amazing Grace" was written for a New Year's Day 1773 sermon. It was printed in England in 1779 in Newton and Cowper's *Olney Hymns*. The song became popular in the United States in the early 19th century. Composer William Walker in 1835 joined the "New Britain" tune to Newton's lyrics, which is the version we know today.

Elvis Presley's adaptation was released in 1972 on his *He Touched Me* album.

AUTHOR'S NOTE

On this writing journey, I've been blessed with many cheerleaders and readers. I'm humbled by the enthusiasm and encouragement I've received from family, friends, colleagues and folks I've met while sharing these Elvis stories. Thanks from the bottom of my heart.

To my editor Joyce Romine of Streamline Communications: thank you for making this sequel better with your thoughtful corrections, edits and suggestions.

Thanks to my advance team, the Piccadilly Power Squad, all avid readers who returned from book one to provide valuable feedback on part two: my loving sister Kati Eddinger; high school bestie Chris Scherting; Florida bestie and teacher Cindy Denner; pinafore pal Becky Reichardt, and talented book designer and friend Katie Robinson.

To my parents and stepparents, brother and baby sis, nieces and nephews, cousins and steps: we're a wacky pack, spread near and far, and I cherish our times together.

To Jeff Barnes: your love was the most precious gift I received following the release of *Waking Up in Graceland*. I love your family and am thrilled about our future together. "A single girl goes to an Elvis festival to sell books and meets a single Elvis"—who could have imagined! Thanks for your unfailing support of my writing.

To my dearest friends—you know who you are—we've walked some wonderful journeys together, from grade school, high school, college, Florida, St. Louis and more. You mean so much to me and I treasure all of the good times and laughter.

Thanks to Laura Jones and Messenger Print Group for another excellent printing experience.

To Priscilla and Lisa Marie Presley, thanks for sharing Elvis with the rest of us. May he continue to live on through the love of fans for many generations.

To my Elvis friends: we're a super-sized high school of fanatical fans and hunky ETAs, with global reach and *the very best reunions*. Our hearts are connected through love of Elvis and his music, and you honor me with each page turn.

BIBLIOGRAPHY

These books helped my research for this novel:

Cocke, Marian J.
I Called Him Babe, 1979.

Garr, Gillian G.
100 Things Elvis Fans Should Know and Do Before They Die, 2014.

Juanico, June.
Elvis In the Twilight of Memory, 1997.

Klein, George with Chuck Crisafulli.
Elvis: My Best Man, 2010.

Nichopoulos, George, M.D. with Rose Clayton Phillips.
The King and Dr. Nick, 2009.

Presley, Priscilla Beaulieu with Sandra Harmon.
Elvis and Me, 1985.

Rooks, Nancy with Jim Cox.
Inside Graceland, 2005.

Schilling, Jerry with Chuck Crisafulli.
Me and a Guy Named Elvis, 2006.

Stanley, David E. with Frank Coffey.
The Elvis Encyclopedia, 2013.

West, Sonny with Marshall Terrill.
Elvis: Still Taking Care of Business, 2007.

ABOUT THE AUTHOR

Kelly Peach has spent her career stringing words into stories. For 30 years, she has written and produced for news, advertising, videos, public relations, corporate communications and more. Kelly won an Emmy for producing a local prime time TV special. For 12 years, she has devoted her writing talents to the mission to end homelessness at St. Patrick Center, where she is Senior Director of Communications.

Kelly lives in her hometown of St. Louis, Missouri. This is her second novel.